PU

Arriving at their great-aunt Hetty's to spend the summer, Tom and Rosa become aware that Hetty's cottage is being watched by Jake Florey from the Manor. Then Rosa has strange, frightening dreams of someone trying to break into the loft of the cottage. They realize something is definitely wrong when they encounter an aggressive Jake and then his even more aggressive father, Giles Florey.

However, it is only when they spend a day at the seaside that they begin to get a glimmer of what might be the cause of these odd events. For there Rosa, by the strangest coincidence, meets an old fortune-teller who tells her that she must find something called The Gift. But what is it and why has Rosa been chosen to save it?

With their young friend, Jamie, Tom and Rosa determine to unravel the secret. But they realize they are not the only ones trying to find The Gift.

In this exciting and original adventure story, the children face great danger and discover extraordinary powers before they reach the dramatic and mysterious climax of their quest.

Rachel Dixon was born in Bristol and trained as a teacher at Westminster College of Education, Oxford. She then taught music and general subjects at an Oxford middle school. She is now a full-time writer and mother, living in Oxford.

Also by Rachel Dixon

THE FOX OF SKELLAND
THE MARSHMALLOW EXPERIMENT
MAX AND THE FIRE CRYSTALS

Rachel Dixon
Black Nest

Illustrated by
Neil Reed

PUFFIN BOOKS

PUFFIN BOOKS

Published by the Penguin Group
Penguin Books Ltd, 27 Wrights Lane, London W8 5TZ, England
Penguin Books USA Inc., 375 Hudson Street, New York, New York 10014, USA
Penguin Books Australia Ltd, Ringwood, Victoria, Australia
Penguin Books Canada Ltd, 10 Alcorn Avenue, Toronto, Ontario, Canada M4V 3B2
Penguin Books (NZ) Ltd, 182–190 Wairau Road, Auckland 10, New Zealand

Penguin Books Ltd, Registered Offices: Harmondsworth, Middlesex, England

First published by Viking Kestrel 1989
Published in Puffin Books 1990
3 5 7 9 10 8 6 4 2

Printed in England by Clays Ltd, St Ives plc
Filmset in 10/12pt Linotron Meridien

For Tony

ONE

Tanglewild looked like everybody's dream cottage. It was a pretty building with walls and tiles of Gloucestershire stone. Wistaria tangled around the front door, chintz curtains hung at the windows and there was a dip in the front doorstep made by generations of feet. The garden was a mass of colour, a butterflies' paradise held in by a mossy drystone wall. It was at the end of a narrow road called Gozzards Reach on the outskirts of Nettlesfield. Beyond it was Swallow Lane, an earth track that meandered between tall trees up the steep valley side.

You could forget your worries in a place like that.

Tom and Rosa Howell were spending the summer there with their great-aunt, Hetty Fletcher. As usual they were given the back bedrooms. Each room had a single brass bedstead with lumpy mattress, leaden bolster and faded patchwork quilt. Apart from a rag rug apiece, the undulating wooden floors were bare. Many photographs and paintings adorned the walls and the dressing-tables were covered with little china figures, pots of everlasting flowers and interesting wooden boxes.

Rosa's bed was under her window. She was kneeling on it, peering out through her mother's binoculars, when Tom knocked on the connecting door between their rooms.

Rat-at-at-at.

They had agreed years ago that neither brother nor sister would enter the other room unannounced and four knocks was the signal.

'Come in,' called Rosa, without turning.

'How's it look?' said Tom, envious because he had no binoculars.

'Great,' said Rosa. 'Chestnut's in the paddock up Swallow Lane and she's as lovely as ever. Nettlebury Manor looks the same; pity it's not close enough to see anything very interesting.'

'What else?'

'I can see Broom lurking in the catmint by the pond. She must be after Hetty's goldfish.'

'What about Black Nest?'

This was a cottage a little way down the lane and was of the same design as Tanglewild.

Why Black Nest?
That was something to do with its past.

In it lived Dora Bishop. Rosa and Tom were very wary of her. She was a simple, nervous woman but, with careless handling, could become strangely aggressive.

2

Rosa could see into the garden.

'The chicken-shed has nearly collapsed,' she said, 'Dora's bloomers are on the line – the same ones as last year – and Mad Bonzo is chewing something disgusting.' Dora's dog was the size of a labrador, with black shaggy fur, oversized floppy ears and very little brain.

As Tom climbed up beside Rosa he noticed a flash of light from near the river.

'Give us a go with the glasses,' he said. 'There's something shiny over there.'

Rosa trained the binoculars along the river's edge, stopping when she saw something metallic. It was beside three pollarded willows.

'It's only an old washing-machine,' she said.

Then she saw something move a little way along the river bank, and trained the glasses on the place. Squatting in the reeds was a youth. There were two dark shapes beside him – probably dogs – and he was holding something to his eyes.

'There's Jake Florey,' she said. 'And he's got binoculars.' Jake lived with his father, Giles Florey, in Nettlebury Manor.

Tom snatched the glasses from her.

'Got him,' he said, hastily focusing. 'He's got binoculars all right and – of all the cheek – they're pointing at us!'

Hetty called them down for tea. (She preferred the children to call her Hetty now they were older.) Sun streamed into the large kitchen. A plate of newly baked cherry scones stood on the scrubbed pine table, beside a big pot of tea.

'Mmm, Hetty's specials!' said Tom.

'Hands washed first, please,' said Hetty. Rosa filled the bowl from the little Ascot heater and sniffed the bar of soap. It was a gritty herbal soap that Hetty made herself.

'Tom next,' said Hetty, lifting down three flowery cups from the dresser. 'Have you both unpacked?'

The children exchanged guilty looks.

'Nearly,' said Tom.

Hetty gave him a penetrating look that made him go pink.

'No,' said Rosa, 'but we'll do it better when we've had one of your delicious scones.'

'Go on with you,' said Hetty.

She beamed at them. It was lovely to have youngsters in the house again. Not that they *were* so young now. They seemed so tall and straight, and each had their father's golden hair.

'What did you see out of the window?' she said. 'Anything interesting?'

'Yes,' said Tom.

'*Very*,' said Rosa.

It was good to be at Tanglewild again. Nothing changed. Hetty was the same; small and old but with a reassuring spring in her step and a comfortable firmness in her voice. She dressed carefully, always covering her clothes with a clean floral overall while working. Her smooth grey hair was swept back into a neat bun, which was dotted with hairpins like pins in a pincushion.

They drank hot tea and ate far too many of the crumbly scones. Nobody said much until Broom the cat sauntered in through the back door with her grey tail held high and pollen on her nose.

'She's been after butterflies again,' said Hetty, tousling the animal's head.

'Broom never looks any older,' said Tom. 'How long have you had her?'

'Long enough,' said Hetty. 'And she could tell a few tales.'

'*If* cats could talk,' laughed Rosa.

4

Broom jumped on to Rosa's lap, gripping through her cotton skirt with sharp claws.

'You'd love to talk to me, wouldn't you?' said Rosa, cradling the animal's silky head. Broom lifted her head and peered up into Rosa's face with eyes like deep pools. For a second it seemed she understood.

'You've a way with animals,' said Hetty. 'Just like your Grandma Connie had with people.'

After tea the children persuaded Hetty to get out the old photograph box. They laughed at the faded pictures of Hetty as a girl, particularly the holiday snaps of her at Westcombe-on-Sea wearing a floppy sun-hat. She had been slender and beautiful in her twenties. Rosa particularly liked a picture of her leaning against the front porch of Tanglewild beside Grandma Connie (then thirty). They could almost have been twins.

'Do you still miss Grandma?' asked Tom. The sisters had lived together for years.

'Yes, I do, even though she's been gone thirteen years this August. You were a baby then and Rosa hadn't been born. Mind you, I know Connie's about the place. She always liked to keep an eye on things did our Connie. That snap was taken the summer before she married your grandfather.'

'And moved to Hampton Leonard,' said Tom. 'We came through there on the way. Mum says it's not a bit like when she was a girl.'

'Raised your mother there, they did. They had twenty happy years before your Grandpa Harold was taken from her. She was lost without him.'

'Is that why she came to live with you?' said Rosa.

'She knew she was always welcome here did our Connie. I was alone by that time. I never married so it was me that stayed here with our mother, Winifred, and later nursed her through her last few years. A full-time job it was; she was like a baby at the end, but I never resented a minute of it. It was nice to have Connie in the house after a few years by myself, especially as we'd always been close sisters.'

'What about our mum?'

'She was off at university then. She was a bright girl. She soon met your dad and never really wanted to come back to Gloucestershire.'

Tom and Rosa knew the story off by heart but never tired of it. Rosa stared intently at the picture, trying to absorb some of its atmosphere. One corner of it had been bent over for so many years that it had fallen off completely.

'That's where the cat was sitting,' she said. 'It looked just like Broom. She must be older than we thought!'

Hetty gave her a strange look.

'How did you know that?' she said. 'The corner fell off that snap long before *you* ever saw it.'

Rosa shrugged.

'I expect you told me,' she said.

'This won't get your cases unpacked,' said Hetty. 'Off you go while I wash the pots. And when you've finished there's the peas to pick for supper.'

Unpacking was not easy at Hetty's because there were very few places to put what you had unpacked. One small drawer was empty in the pine chest in Tom's bedroom. He crammed as many pairs of pants, socks and T-shirts as he could in there, hung his camera and sponge-bag over a brass bedknob and put his books, torch and pyjama bottoms under the bolster. (He'd forgotten to get the pyjama top from the airing cupboard, but a T-shirt would do instead.) He hid his Walkman in the bed because he'd told Rosa he wouldn't need it at Tanglewild.

Anything else remained in his case, which was pushed under the bed.

Rosa had brought several wire coat-hangers for her dresses and trousers. These were hung on the hook on the bedroom door. T-shirts, jumpers, socks and canvas shoulderbag went over the end of the bedstead and her torch, nightie and Ordnance Survey map under the bolster. Her underwear, books, penknife and an envelope from their mother containing emergency money went under the bed in her case.

Before she found a place for the binoculars Rosa had another look out of the window. First she looked along the valley from Nettlebury Manor to the village, and then up the valley side to Stinchampton Common. She could pick out several people along the top, some on horses and a few playing golf. Sweeping the glasses back down to Hetty's garden she saw that Tom had already started picking the peas. Broom was watching him from the top of the drystone wall, occasionally lifting her paw to swipe at a passing butterfly.

The peas were small and sweet and the children ate nearly as many as they saved. When the job was finished they sat under the apple tree at the bottom of the garden. The air there was full of butterflies and the heady scent of lemon balm.

'No Banbury Road car fumes,' said Tom happily.

'And no horrible noises,' said Rosa. 'This beats Oxford. I always think I'm going to miss civilization — you know, television, a loo that flushes first time and carpet in the bathroom — but I never do.'

For supper Hetty had made a herby potato bake, deliciously seasoned with sage and onion, to go with the garden peas. This was followed by cider-lemon sponge and custard. Hetty's elderberry squash made the children giggly, though it was non-alcoholic.

'Your food is so . . . *different*, Hetty,' said Tom. 'It's sort of relaxing in a filling kind of way.' This started them giggling again and Hetty suggested it was time for bed.

'Goodnight, Hetty,' said Rosa. 'I shall sleep like a log.'

'Me too,' said Tom.

But they didn't.

TWO

It was midnight when Tom awoke.

It took him a moment to remember he was at Tanglewild.

The moon shone through the unlined curtains like early-morning sun. He wondered if Rosa was awake and tiptoed across the room to the connecting door.

Rat-at-at-at.

No answer.

He eased open the door. He could see Rosa's bed clearly in the moonlight and knew at once that she was not in it. There was a dip in the bolster where her head had been and the sheets and quilt were pushed back.

He stood in the open doorway for five, maybe ten, minutes. He expected to hear the lavatory flush and Rosa's footsteps on the landing. He felt very tired and his limbs ached with the effort of waiting. The air was strangely heavy. He would lie on his bed for ten minutes and if Rosa had not returned then he would investigate.

Rosa's senses seemed sharper than usual for a dream. She heard tapping noises from above her . . . it couldn't be mice or bats; it was too persistent, almost mechanical . . . she'd just have to look to see if the trap into the loft was open, though she was sure Hetty hadn't been in there for years.

The rag rug felt cool under her toes as she stepped out of bed. The moon shone brightly through the thin curtains so she could easily see her way to the door.

The tapping continued.

Rat-at-at-at.

She turned the cool ceramic handle of her bedroom door and stepped out on to the landing, closing the door behind her. Tom's and Hetty's doors were opposite each other near the end of the landing. Both were closed. Beyond them, fixed to a beam, stood a wooden loft ladder. Above it was the trap, also closed.

The tapping had stopped.

Rosa waited for five minutes, maybe ten, listening there on the landing, until fatigue overtook her. She would lie on her bed for a few minutes until it started again.

THREE

Rosa awoke to the smell of cooked breakfast. She got out of bed and chose some clothes: a cotton T-shirt, trousers and cardigan, as they would walk up Swallow Lane this morning. As she laced up her trainers she listened for sounds from Tom's room.

It was silent.

She knocked on the connecting door.

Rat-at-at-at.

'Come in.'

His voice was muffled by the bedclothes. Rosa went in and tugged at a corner of the quilt.

'Come on, lazy. Breakfast's cooking. Smell it?'

He sat up.

'Where were you in the night?' he said.

'In bed.'

'Not when I came looking for you.'

'You've been having dreams,' said Rosa. 'I thought you never remembered them.'

Tom looked puzzled.

'I don't usually,' he said.

'I had one too. There was something tapping in the loft . . . and I saw a loft ladder that's never been there before,' said Rosa. 'It was a bit spooky.'

'The ghost of Grandma Connie,' said Tom.

'Don't be silly,' said Rosa. 'And get up. If you're not down in ten minutes I'll eat your breakfast.'

Hetty was frying parsnip pancakes and eggs.

'Set the table would you, dear?' she said. 'I've cooked your favourite. Going up Swallow Lane, are you?'

Rosa nodded.

'You'll need a good breakfast inside you, then.'

Rosa lifted the patterned plates off the dresser and put them to warm on the Aga.

'I'm starving,' she said.

'Busy dreams?' said Hetty. She slid a well-cooked egg on to one of the plates, leaving a greasy track across the rim.

'Will you come with us up the lane?' said Rosa.

'I've not got the stamina these days, dear, and you don't want to be bothered with an old lady like me while you're here. I've plenty of jobs to do; there's the weeding to see to and I must collect some dandelions from along the Reach.'

'Have you got a rabbit?'

'No, dear. They're for Lotty Carpenter. The poor dear loves to play the piano but she's been feeling a bit rheumaticky lately. I told her a glass a day of my dandelion infusion would have her to rights in no time.'

Hetty liked to be busy; it was the only way to keep healthy. She loved growing things, knew the name of

12

every plant in her garden and added new varieties whenever she could. The herbs were used for cooking, fragrant bath mix, infusions and herb pillows. She also mixed lotions to soothe cuts and bruises, and potions for the relief of hay-fever and indigestion. From the flowers she made lavender bags, which she delicately sewed and embroidered by hand, pot-pourri, posies of everlasting flowers, pomanders and scented soaps.

The air was warm and damp when Tom and Rosa left the cottage. The grey clouds promised a shower so they had tied their lightweight anoraks around their waists. The lane wound upwards beside Mr Cairns's cow pasture. The cows had come right up to the fence to shelter under the beech trees. They munched rhythmically and flicked flies off their backs with dirty tails.

'Let's not go right up to the top today,' said Rosa. 'If we take the left fork at the rotten elm stump we could go into Chestnut's paddock. I'd like to look at Tanglewild through the binoculars. Hetty said she'd wave her overall if she saw our red anoraks.'

Chestnut was not in her paddock.

'Someone must be riding her,' said Rosa. 'I wish *I* had a horse.'

'Me too,' said Tom. 'But we can't afford it. Besides, they're a nuisance.'

'How do you know?'

'Lisa Copcutt. She's mad on her horse. I invited her to the ice rink after school *twice* last term and she said she couldn't come because she was so busy with the silly animal.'

'What's it called?'

'Pest, I expect.'

Looking down from the middle of the paddock they had a magnificent view. On their left Swallow Lane curved down to Gozzards Reach, past Tanglewild and Black Nest into the centre of the village. Around the village square were the old stone houses, some of them shops. Along the main street, behind Bluebell Wood, were the grey backs of tiny terraced cottages. They made Tanglewild seem large. Some modern buildings, like Hopkins' Post Office, were beginning to fan out from the centre, though it was unlikely many more planning applications would be accepted. Over to their right the valley began to narrow. The land around the river and Nettlebury Manor belonged to Giles Florey. This and the wooded acres beyond would always be protected from development.

Rosa got out the binoculars.

'Any sign of Hetty?' asked Tom.

'No. I don't think she ever remembers to look out for us.'

'There's someone on a bike by Tanglewild, though. Who is it?'

'It's the postman. He's delivering something to Hetty. A parcel I think. She said she was expecting some new embroidery threads. She had to order them from Gloucester.'

'Let me have a go.'

Rosa released the glasses and rested on a springy tussock of grass. A grey mist of rain was beginning to move down the valley. It would reach them in minutes but she didn't mind. Rain seemed cleaner at Nettlesfield.

'Well!' said Tom. 'Of all the nerve. There's Jake Florey at his tricks again. He's got his glasses out again and I'll swear they're trained on Hetty's cottage. Now he's put them down. He's writing something in a notebook.'

'Has he got his umbrella?' said Rosa. 'Because if he hasn't he's about to get drenched.'

'No, he hasn't,' laughed Tom. 'And serve the snooper right. Have a look at him. He's running back to the Manor and there isn't any shelter for miles!'

FOUR

Jake Florey had instructions to watch the cottages on Gozzards Reach for a week. It was Tuesday – three more days to go – but he'd had enough. The boredom was bad enough, but it was the thought of what he *could* have been doing that made him angry. This morning he had seen Mr Cairns riding his horse down Swallow Lane; he should have been with *his* horse Blade instead of skulking about in a patch of water reeds. It irritated him to see that those Howell kids were back again; they were far too nice for his liking. It would help if his father would tell him what he was looking for. He could only assume that he was up to no good and, if that was the case, he was sure that he had not seen anything that could possibly be of interest.

Jake's notes for the morning were as follows:

7.30 a.m. Hetty Fletcher lets cat in
7.45 a.m. Dora Bishop lets dog out
7.46 a.m. Dog goes berserk
7.59 a.m. Dog barks at tree
8.05 a.m. H.F. curtains in back bedroom (left) open
8.13 a.m. H.F. curtains in back bedroom (right) open
9.03 a.m. Dog stops barking – called in for food?
9.08 a.m. Howell children walk up Swallow Lane, go in Cairns's paddock
9.20 a.m. They have binoculars – might have seen me
9.25 a.m. Postman carries parcel towards front H.F. house
9.28 a.m. Howel children put on anoraks

Spots of rain began to drop on the page. Jake snapped the book shut and cursed. He had forgotten his anorak and it would take at least fifteen minutes to get back to the Manor.

'Come on, you stupid hounds,' he said to the dogs.

The dogs, two sleek black labradors, cowered. Jake strode off in a vain attempt to avoid a drenching and they slunk reluctantly after him.

Nettlebury Manor was a large squarish building spoiled by the addition of an ugly extension. The interior, which could have been attractive, lacked the cosiness of the village homes. The hallway and central staircase, though elaborately decorated, felt cool and unwelcoming and the Cotswold stone exterior looked flat and dull. The façade was so gloomy that the Virginia creeper had perished and withered there, its dead leaves flapping damply in the driving rain.

The bedraggled boy was not received sympathetically by his father.

'What are you doing here, boy?' he said. 'I thought I sent you on an errand. It was simple enough, wasn't it? Watch those cottages for a week I said, and that is what I meant.'

The dogs padded mud on to the wooden floor of the entrance hall.

'And get those repulsive hounds out of here while I'm talking to you.'

'I came to get my anorak,' said Jake. 'It's pouring out there.'

'I know it's pouring out there. I don't need you to tell me *that*. I can see the rain. What I *do* need to know is what the residents of the cottages are up to, and I think there is going to be half an hour missing from your record of this morning unless you get back to your look-out spot very quickly.'

Jake opened his mouth to speak. He wanted to ask what he was meant to be looking for. Surely he could trust his own son? Giles Florey marched crossly up the stairs.

Jake closed his mouth. What was the point? He picked up his green waterproof and a large fishing umbrella from the ornate hall stand, scowled at his reflection in the dirty mirror and turned to leave.

His father called after him: 'I always knew you'd be no good. You take after your mother.'

As Jake squelched across the fields down to his look-out post by the river fury welled up inside him. His father had no right to talk about his mother like that. Water began to seep into his left wellington. Someone would pay for his discomfort. The Howell children had better keep out of his way.

FIVE

Rosa was dreaming.

She was in a large black tent. An electric light bulb dangled down from the ridge. Spotlighted beneath it was a wooden table on which stood an old typewriter surrounded with piles of dusty books. Around the table was darkness, smooth oppressive darkness. A piece of paper was in the typewriter. Rosa tried to walk round to read it but her feet felt too heavy and the air too thick.

There was a chair by the table . . . **with someone sitting in it***.*

'It's all right. It looks like Hetty . . . But why is she frightened? She's got to put the light out. She's listening for something . . . waiting for someone . . . but not because she wants them to come.'

Rosa backed towards the edge of the tent and felt cool boards. It wasn't a tent. It was a loft. There was a dark blue rectangle up there. It was the skylight.

'Hetty's looking out of the skylight . . . **what's that creaking noise***? . . . Someone is trying to get in . . . someone who wants to harm Hetty.'*

Someone had hold of Rosa . . . shaking her shoulders . . . a face peered into hers . . . **'Let go! Let me go!'**

'It's only me, you idiot,' said Tom. 'You were wandering about in your nightie. I think you've been sleepwalking.'

'I don't sleepwalk,' said Rosa crossly.

'Well, whatever you were doing you looked pretty scared. What's going on?'

They were standing on the landing outside Rosa's room. The trapdoor to the loft was firmly closed and no sound came from the loft or from Hetty's room.

'Shh,' whispered Rosa. 'Come into my room and I'll explain.'

They sat on the edge of Rosa's bed with the quilt wrapped round their shoulders.

'I was in the loft,' said Rosa. 'It was hard to tell what was happening, but Hetty was in there and she was frightened.'

'A nightmare,' said Tom. 'But that doesn't explain why you were wandering about. That's the second night you've been out of your room.'

Rosa looked puzzled.

'Last night. Remember? I came to see you and your bed was empty.'

'I thought it was a dream,' said Rosa. 'I was on the landing. There was a ladder up to the loft.'

She looked scared.

'Don't worry,' said Tom, squeezing her shoulders. 'People don't come to any harm sleepwalking; I bet it's only happened because you're in a different house. And the dream's nothing to worry about. You always were a bit of a dreamer.'

Rosa decided not to mention the typewriter, and the creaking noise. Yet.

SIX

Tom knocked on Rosa's door before going down to breakfast. She was already dressed and sat cross-legged on her bed poring over an Ordnance Survey map of the area. She handed Tom the binoculars.

'Look over towards the river and tell me what you see,' she said. 'It's still misty, but I think you'll spot him.'

'Jake Florey's there again!' said Tom. 'Who does he think he is? It's time we sorted him out.'

'Right.'

'But how?'

'I'll show you.'

Rosa wore a determined expression that Tom knew

well and he felt a twinge of excitement. It was sometimes hard to believe that she was a year younger than he was.

'Look at this map,' she said. 'Here's Gozzards Reach. That dotted line is Swallow Lane and there's Stinchampton Beacon at the top. You follow?'

'Course I do. I'm not stupid.'

'Good. Now look at Nettlebury Manor. Here's where the river goes through Florey's meadow. This is where Jake Florey seems to spend his time at the moment.'

'That's *just* where he is,' said Tom. 'By the sharp curve in the river. Pity we can't get over there. I'd like to have a word with him.'

'I think I may be able to help you there,' said Rosa.

Tom detected a note of triumph in her voice.

'Look at this dotted line and tell me where it starts,' she said.

'Gozzards Reach by the look of it. Somewhere near Dora's cottage.'

'Exactly. And where does it lead?'

'To the river. No, *over* the river – there must be a bridge. Then it goes alongside the river, over the field next to the Manor, across the river again and up the valley side. It must come out at that viewing point on the Stinchampton Road.'

'Yes,' said Rosa smugly. 'A public pathway straight through Florey's land. Isn't it great? We could walk right past Jake Florey and there's nothing he can do about it.'

'Brilliant!' said Tom. 'This map's recent so the path is sure to be there. It's funny that there's no sign though. There's always been a very clear one pointing up to the beacon.'

'I bet I know why there's no sign,' said Rosa grimly. 'It's because the Floreys don't want anybody wandering through their land. And wouldn't it be interesting to know why?'

'Yes,' agreed Tom. 'It's not as if they're short of space. Let's check out the path after breakfast. What's Hetty got on the menu today, I wonder?'

Rosa sniffed the air expertly.

'Redcurrant waffles and scrambled eggs with chopped parsley and chives,' she said.

Broom followed Tom and Rosa down Gozzards Reach towards the village, but only as far as Black Nest. She stopped there to rub her nose against the stone wall and a dusty cobweb stuck over her ear like a miniature hairnet.

'Come on, puss,' called Rosa.

But Broom would go no further. Instead she sprang on to the top of the wall, wobbling for a moment on a loose stone.

'According to the map,' said Tom, 'the path leaves Gozzards Reach down here on the right . . . but where? It's all hedge until the crossroads.'

'It must be just past Dora's garden,' said Rosa. 'If you look at the map it can't be much further east.'

She walked back and stroked Broom's shiny back.

'I'm sure *you've* been down the track,' she said. 'Tell Rosa where it is.'

Tom sat on the verge. 'Don't be long,' he said.

'Don't listen to him,' she whispered. Broom's throat vibrated with rich purrs.

'It would help if some idiot hadn't moved the sign,' said Tom.

Broom stiffened suddenly. She stared intently down the side of Dora's cottage towards her back garden and swished her tail. Rosa followed her gaze. Mad Bonzo had been let out and was snuffling his way towards them, pushing his big wet nose along the earth like a vacuum-cleaner nozzle. But Broom seemed to show more interest

22

in Dora Bishop, who hobbled out carrying dripping underwear in one hand and a grubby cloth peg-bag in the other. The washing-line looped from an apple tree to a white-painted post. Dora hung the peg-bag over a rectangle of metal that was pinned to the top of the post and selected two wooden pegs. She held one in her teeth while draping her long combinations over the line. She looked startled to see the children.

'What you looking at?' she said suspiciously.

The peg wobbled up and down in her mouth as she spoke.

'Just saying what a good drying day it is, Miss Bishop,' said Rosa.

'That's why I'm hanging out my washing,' said Dora proudly. '*And* I've hung the bolster out of my window to get an airing. I can always tell a good drying day.'

'Not everybody can do that,' said Tom kindly.

She beamed happily. The peg fell to the ground, and because it was no longer in her mouth Dora forgot about the washing and shuffled into her cottage.

'Look at the washing post,' said Rosa. 'Does it remind you of something?'

'A piece of wood?'

'Don't be silly. Look at the bit on the top.'

'Aren't they always like that?'

'Not that I know of. It's like a signpost. I bet it's the one for the pathway. Dora must have "borrowed" it for her washing!'

'Here she comes again,' said Tom. 'She's remembered her undies. Wait until she goes in and we'll see if we can get through the hedge. She doesn't seem too bad today, but she might turn nasty if she sees what we're up to. The path must be round here. She can't have carried that thing far.'

They waved at Dora and walked off as if they were

leaving. Mad Bonzo flopped his silly head over the wall and gazed affectionately at Broom with bloodshot eyes. Broom gently touched her pink nose to his before jumping down from the wall. She walked back to Hetty's cottage with her tail curved in a neat question mark.

'Thanks, Broom,' whispered Rosa.

By looking through the hedge the children could see the remains of a stone wall, and set in it, not far from Dora's garden, was a crumbling stone stile.

'That must be the way through,' said Tom. 'It's so overgrown it can't have been used for ages.'

Though the hedge was thick it had not rooted beside the stile and by prising back the main branches and flattening down the cow parsley and long grasses below, it was possible to tunnel through. Tom went first.

'Pull up the grass behind you so we shan't be followed,' he said. 'And when we're over the stile let's keep our heads down. We don't want Dora to spot us.'

As they made their way to the end of Dora's garden Bonzo sensed that something was going on and began to bark excitedly. He ran up and down on the other side of the wall, occasionally leaping high into the air. As this resembled his normal behaviour Dora Bishop suspected nothing.

They crossed two fields keeping to the east side of the walls and hedges so Jake wouldn't see them coming. They stopped for breath in the birch copse. Beyond it was the meadow and river.

'Let's look at the map,' said Rosa. 'We want to be sure we know our right of way. I think those wooden posts in the reeds must be part of the bridge. If we cross there and keep to the river's edge we should be all right. We'll be in his view when we come out of the trees though, so let's hide the map.'

Tom slid the map into his jeans pocket.

Rosa heard a rustling noise in the birch branches. 'Oh *do* look, Tom,' she whispered. 'A dear little squirrel.' The startled animal leapt on to the next tree, its grey tail billowing out like a shaken duvet, and eyed Rosa curiously. Rosa made clicking noises with her tongue and the animal put its head on one side. 'Come, come,' whispered Rosa. Her voice was like velvet. The little creature scrambled down the tree and hopped within a metre of her feet. 'Sorry, no food,' said Rosa gently.

Tom laughed and the squirrel scuttled to the base of the tree. 'Off you go, then,' said Rosa. The animal gave her a sharp look before running up into the leaves and Rosa knew that if she had been alone it would have come to her hand. She would have some nuts in her pocket next time.

By peering between the trees Tom could see that Jake was still there. He was crouching by the curve in the river, looking towards the cottages through his binoculars. His dogs sat beside him, sleek and alert. Though Tom had few qualms about confronting Jake he felt slightly uneasy about the dogs. He'd had unpleasant experiences with dogs while delivering free newspapers in Oxford.

'How shall we play this?' said Rosa.

'As far as *he's* concerned we are exploring the local countryside. And if he turns nasty we can point out that we are on a public right of way.'

As they walked out on to the meadow a kestrel hovered above them, pointing its fanned tail down to stabilize itself. Rosa turned her binoculars to watch it.

'See it dive,' she said.

'I'm watching Jake Florey,' said Tom with satisfaction. 'He's spotted us. I bet he's furious.'

The bird swooped down in stages, half closing its wings

for its final pounce. Its strong wings beat against the grass for a moment until it overpowered its victim. Then it soared up across the sky to Swallow Wood.

The bridge was where they had expected it to be. It was a simple wooden affair with a flimsy handrail. The river was no more than three metres wide and looked narrower because of the tall reeds growing there. Tom pushed a long stick down to test the depth. The water was shallow but the mud beneath it was soft and deep. It dripped off the stick like melted chocolate.

Once over the river they looked back towards the cottages.

'He must have a good view of us from here,' said Tom. 'I bet he can see into every room.'

'Especially at night when the lights are on,' said Rosa. She shivered at the thought.

Jake stood now. He was about a hundred metres along the bank, beyond three pollarded willows. As they walked towards him he turned to face them, his hands on his hips.

Tom noticed he had grown since last summer, especially his arms. His black hair, which had been short, now surrounded his scowling face in a mass of aggressive curls.

Rosa and Tom stopped by the trees. Beside them lay the washing-machine they had seen from their window. Distended lips of black rubber hung out around the circular door.

'Front loader,' said Tom as if it was of any interest. He pulled open the door. 'Act natural,' he whispered as he peered inside.

He found a damp maroon sock in it. It was furry with grey mould.

'Ugh! Put it back,' said Rosa.

'Nylon,' said Tom in his Sherlock Holmes voice. 'Just

as I expected.' It made a soggy noise against the drum as he threw it back in.

Jake did not speak until they were within three metres of him.

'Stop where you are,' he said. His upper lip curled like the perished rubber on the washing-machine.

Rosa and Tom stopped.

'You are trespassing on Nettlebury Manor,' he said nastily. 'So beat it.' He gave a low short whistle and the labradors sprang up, one on either side, alert and ready for instructions. Rosa was impressed by the sleek black creatures, though she suspected they were slightly under-nourished. She noticed their eyes flicker with fear when Jake moved his arms.

Rosa took a step forward.

The dogs growled.

'You're wrong,' she said. 'We're not trespassing.'

'I know a trespasser when I see one,' sneered Jake. 'Leave my land before I have to make you.'

'*Your* land?' said Tom. 'What rubbish.'

'If you look at the map of this area you'll see that we're on a public footway,' said Rosa.

'I've got a copy here if you'd like to check,' said Tom.

'Get off this land before I set the dogs on you,' said Jake. His eyes flashed angrily. He had expected them to be easier to intimidate. They'd grown since last summer, especially the girl.

'We saw you yesterday morning,' said Rosa. 'Pity about the rain. I hope you didn't get too wet.'

Jake saw red.

He slapped the dogs sharply on their flanks and snarled: 'Get them!'

They bounded forward, eyes narrow, lips pulled back above sharp teeth. Tom couldn't move. He watched with horror as Rosa stepped forward. She stretched out her thin arms and the dogs went for her . . .

But as they leapt they saw her face. They stopped for a moment, puzzled. Then their jowls flopped into silly smiles and warm pink tongues came out to lick the friendly face. Rosa cradled the huge creatures in her arms and tickled their ears.

'You darlings,' she said. 'Come on. Come to Rosa.'

And the dogs whimpered in delight at the first affection they had seen for months.

Tom threw back his head and laughed with relief. He was still smiling as Jake strode up to him. Jake grabbed the front of Tom's T-shirt with both hands.

'You think it's funny, do you?' he said, shaking him roughly.

Tom noticed with satisfaction that Jake had a spot on his chin.

'Well, listen to me, Howell, you'd better keep out of my way in the future.'

'Or else?'

'Just don't try it or you'll find out.'

He released Tom, pushing him so hard that he fell to the ground, and strode off towards the Manor without looking at Rosa or his dogs.

The dogs were confused. 'Go on, girls,' whispered Rosa. She gently pushed the poor creatures away. They soon caught up with Jake and padded obediently beside him with their tails down. Rosa flinched as she saw Jake give each of them a sharp kick.

'Come on,' said Tom gently. 'I think we've made our point. Let's go home.

Rosa nodded sadly.

'Are you all right?' she said.

'A bit bruised,' he said, rubbing his elbow. 'I'll have to get Hetty to rub one of her lotions on it.'

SEVEN

The following morning Tom went down to the post office to get stamps, envelopes and brown paper for Hetty. Mrs Hopkins was serving. She was a large, friendly woman with wiry grey hair that sat on her head like a mistake.

'If it isn't young Thomas,' she said as she slipped the crisp stamps under the partition. 'Are you staying with your great-aunt again?'

Tom nodded. He knew from experience that she did not allow much time for answers.

'It hardly seems a week since you were last here,' she continued, 'but you've grown so much it *must* be a year.'

She laughed loudly and her huge bosom wobbled inside her overall.

'I'd like these envelopes and some brown paper, please,' said Tom.

'You'll have to come to the other counter for those,' she said, squeezing herself off her chair. 'I'll give Jamie a call.'

Jamie had heard and came out of the back room. He was a cheerful ginger-haired boy with a dusting of freckles on his nose.

'Come and see how Thomas has grown,' said Mrs Hopkins.

Jamie grinned apologetically.

'You ought to ask him round. You've been mooning about ever since school broke up.'

Mrs Hopkins hauled herself back on to her chair and took an old lady's allowance book.

'All right, Mrs Singh?' she said, deftly pounding the rubber stamp on to a crumpled allowance book. 'How are your ankles, love?' She counted out the money. 'Here you are, dear. Don't forget your book, will you?'

Mrs Singh hobbled painfully out of the shop.

'Poor old soul,' said Mrs Hopkins. 'I can hardly get a word out of her since her husband died.'

She shook her head thoughtfully. Jamie took the money for Tom's paper and envelopes.

'Jamie's best mate's gone abroad for a fortnight. All right for some, isn't it?' said Mrs Hopkins returning her attention to the boys.

'Want to come in the back for a bit?' asked Jamie.

'That's right. You go and play. Sharee should be here any minute to serve. She gets later every day.'

Jamie raised his eyes.

'She still thinks I'm five,' he said, laughing. 'It's a wonder I don't get a bedtime story.'

'Less of your cheek, young man,' she cackled.

*

The back room was a gloomy place, the dullness of its grey walls relieved only by a high window and a door to the backyard. It was used for filing and the storage of stock and cleaning equipment, but one corner was set aside as a rest area with a lumpy armchair and table. On the table were three or four chipped mugs, several used teabags and a small electric kettle.

'It's a bit squalid in here,' said Jamie. 'I'd take you up to the flat, but today is delivery day from the stationers' and I have to listen out for them.'

They made themselves as comfortable as they could; Tom sat on the chair, which felt as though it was stuffed with potatoes, and Jamie on a splintery crate. Jamie tore open a cardboard box and took out two cans of Coke which they drank in silence for a minute.

'Is your sister with you?' said Jamie.

'Yes. She's helping Hetty this morning. She's keen on weeding and a bit of the vegetable patch needs doing. Hetty would do it, only she had another parcel yesterday.'

'Parcel of what?'

'I'm not sure; wool or something. She makes things, you know.'

Jamie looked unimpressed.

'Do you fancy biking over to Sladbury Park this afternoon for a swim?' he said. 'I can lend you my dad's bike. Can your sister get hold of one?'

'Yes, she can borrow Hetty's boneshaker. It'll make a change to cycle. We've only been walking so far.'

'Where have you been? Up Swallow Hill?'

'Yes, and into Nettlebury Manor.'

Jamie's face clouded.

'You're not pally with Jake Florey, are you?' he said.

'Not unless you call *this* being friendly,' said Tom. He showed Jamie the large bruise on his arm. 'That's what I got for taking a stroll along a public right of way.'

'He's no good,' said Jamie grimly. 'I could tell you a few things about the Floreys.'

A horn beeped outside.

'That's Sid with the delivery. I'll see you here about one-thirty. Let yourself out through the shop.'

He unlocked the back door and hurried out.

Tom was curious to know what Jamie had to say about the Floreys. But it would have to wait.

Jamie was sitting on the front step of the shop when Tom and Rosa arrived that afternoon. He held an empty Coke can which he deftly kicked into the nearby rubbish bin, disturbing several wasps.

'Been practising, have you?' said Tom.

The wasps settled on the can, sensing its sweetness.

Jamie eyed Hetty's ancient cycle doubtfully.

'Are you sure you can make it on that?' he said.

Rosa blushed. Jamie was better looking than she remembered.

'We'll take it in turns,' said Tom. 'If you think *this* is bad you should have seen it before we pumped up the tyres.'

He peered down at the balding front tyre and pressed it experimentally.

Rosa nudged him as a filthy Range Rover pulled up. In it were Giles and Jake Florey.

'Don't look now,' she said, 'but a friend of ours has just arrived.'

Jake Florey scowled out at her through the mud-splattered window while his father jumped out and strode up to the shop door. He wore a tweed jacket and leather boots and would have looked quite the country gentleman had it not been for his unruly dark hair, bloodshot eyes and unshaven chin. A knobbly pipe protruded from between his nicotine-stained teeth. He puffed on it impatiently and waited for the children to move away from the door. Tom and Rosa moved aside, but Jamie stood his ground.

'I'm afraid you can't go in,' he said.

'Out of my way,' said Giles roughly.

Jamie smiled at him and pointed to a 'No Smoking' notice on the door. Tom and Rosa watched in admiration and disbelief.

'Let me pass, boy. I only want some stamps and I'm in a hurry.'

'Sorry,' said Jamie.

'I'll only ask you once more,' said Giles.

Rosa felt uneasy and Tom wanted to giggle.

'That *is* smoke coming out of your pipe, isn't it?' asked Jamie innocently.

Unable to control his temper any longer Giles raised his arm . . .

'I'll hold the pipe for you,' said Rosa. Her tone was that of someone offering to help an old lady with her shopping. She stepped between Jamie and Giles and held out her hand.

'I'll not have any of you lot touching *anything* that belongs to me,' he snarled. 'And I don't intend to go in this shop again either.'

'I hope not,' said Rosa, 'if it means resorting to violence . . . and as it looks as if Jake is not "on watch" today you might like to tell him that we are all going swimming this afternoon and should be back about tea-time.'

It wasn't until the Floreys had driven off that Rosa realized she felt dizzy. She sank down on to the cool step. Through the buzzing noise in her ears she could hear the boys congratulating her. She tried to smile and wondered if she would ever tell them the truth; how could she explain that although she was glad she had intervened, she had been driven to do so by a force that she did not begin to understand. She had experienced the same feeling with Jake's dogs the day before. And again it had left her physically drained.

'I won't go swimming if you don't mind,' she said. 'I don't feel very well.'

Jamie looked concerned.

'I'll take the boneshaker into our backyard,' he said. 'You shouldn't ride it home. Tom can wheel it back later.'

Tom walked Rosa as far as the square.

'I think I'll go with Jamie,' he said. He made a pile of dust in the gutter with the toe of his shoe. 'Apart from anything else I'd like to know what he's got against the Floreys. You don't risk being hit without a reason.'

'No?' said Rosa grimly. 'So why did *I* risk it?'

'Because you're barmy,' he said, trying to make her smile.

'And why did he say "any of you lot"? Is he just a snob or has he got something against Hetty? Do you think we should talk to her about it?'

'We'll tackle that one later,' said Tom. He squeezed her arm. 'Don't you do anything rash. Not today anyway.'

Rosa walked up Gozzards Reach and the jabbing of sharp pebbles through the soles of her trainers revived her.

As he watched her go Tom thought that he would never understand her. She was such a funny mixture at the moment: sometimes vulnerable, sometimes extraordinarily strong and on occasions downright weird.

The water in Sladbury Park swimming-pool was refreshingly cool. Tom had found the hilly ride exhausting after the flat roads of Oxford, so the boys only swam a few lengths before lounging on some enormous fish-shaped floats left in the water by the Mothers' and Toddlers' Swimming Group.

'Have you had problems with Florey before?' said Tom.

'Not me,' said Jamie, 'but my aunt used to work as housekeeper at the Manor until a few months ago, when Giles gave her the push.'

'That's rough,' said Tom. 'And she hadn't a clue why?'

'Only the fact that he became even more unbearable to work for after his old father snuffed it. That was a few weeks before she was sacked. Apparently he spent hours rooting about in old Florey's room and came out really moody and a bit violent. What's he done to you?'

'It's not so much him as Jake. We've seen him watching the cottage through binoculars.'

'I'd like to bet that his dad's put him up to that,' said Jamie. 'He's too pathetic to think of it himself. What do you think the idiot is looking for?'

'I don't know,' said Tom. 'But I intend to find out.'

A man bellowed at them from the pool side.

'Geroff the floats, you 'ooligans. The Mothers' Group 'eld a raffle to pay for 'em and it wasn't so as the likes of you could wear 'em out.'

EIGHT

*R*osa was frightened. Someone was coming. Someone evil. He wanted information but she would
not give it . . .

'Where is it, woman? Tell me where it is and
you'll not get hurt.'

It was misty out there. Ghostly.

'If you don't tell me where it is I shall have to come
and get it.'

He'd sent them, but they hadn't found it. What a
clever idea to put it in the loft. Did he really expect to
find valuables in the cottage?

'We'll be back . . . we'll be back.'

They would come tonight . . . in the mist. But
she'd be ready . . . lock the doors and hide in the
loft. He'd never get in.

**'He's out there. And he's not alone. Don't
let him in!'**

'I should never have taken it. Best tell the truth
. . . don't be angry with me.'

**'He's got a ladder. I hear it creaking. Help
me!'**

Rosa was cold. The dreams were getting too real. She
had not just dreamed the fear; she had *known* it. She sat
up in bed and was comforted a little by familiar shadows;
a posy of dried flowers in the corner, the binoculars and
canvas bag over the end of the bed and the outline of the
chest of drawers. She felt for her torch and shone it on
her watch. It was 1.12 a.m.

Something made her look out of the window. It was dark and cloudy, but there was a red glow in the meadow by the river. It was a bonfire. She reached for the binoculars and could just make out the black shape of someone throwing something into the flames.

She did not know that in a window of Nettlebury Manor someone else stood, watching.

NINE

Rosa struggled out of bed the following morning. Her limbs ached and her head felt fuzzy. She tried to pull her clothes on but the effort was too much and when she tried to call Tom her voice was a mere croak. Somehow she got to his door and knocked, holding on to the cool door handle to balance herself. But he wasn't there. He must be downstairs. There was a dull thudding behind her sore eyes. She knelt on the floorboards, picked up one of the trainers that lay pigeon-toed by the chest and pounded it urgently on the floor. And then she was going down ... floating, until her cheek rested on the dry wood. The last thing she saw was a spider scuttling under the skirting-board.

*

It was Hetty's icy hand on her forehead that brought her round. She saw two fat fish swimming from side to side.

'What's all this?' said one of them.

. . . It was a face . . . Hetty's face.

'Is she all right?' said the other.

. . . Tom.

'She will be,' said Hetty. 'Let's get her back on that bed and you can stay with her while I make balm tea. That'll get the temperature down and then we can see what's what.'

So they lifted her up, one on either arm, and Rosa tried to make her heavy legs walk across the floor. The sheets, still damp from her fever, made her shiver.

'I'll make a nice hot-water-bottle, too,' said Hetty. 'And no talking for a while. The child is exhausted.'

'I think it's all right if I talk to *you*,' said Tom when Hetty had gone. 'Did I tell you how good the pool was? You could come next time. It wasn't nearly as crowded as the Ferry Pool.'

Rosa tried to keep her eyes open. If she fell asleep she might dream.

'Jamie has asked us round for tea today, so you've got to get better.'

Rosa heard Hetty's footsteps on the landing. She wanted to tell Tom about the nightmare and the fire in the meadow.

'Here's your bottle,' said Hetty. 'The tea's got to infuse for another ten minutes. I'll bring it up when it's ready. I shall pop in some lemon and honey to make it taste nice. I think she's best left now, Tom. Rest is a great healer.'

Apart from waking for sips of balm tea Rosa slept for most of the morning without dreaming. She felt much better by lunchtime and managed to eat scrambled egg and slices of pear. Tom was allowed to see her after lunch.

'I got you this magazine,' he said. 'I thought you'd like the poster of Madonna and here's my Walkman in case you fancy some music. I know I said I wouldn't need it here, but you never know when there's going to be an emergency.'

Rosa tried to smile.

'Cheer up,' said Tom. 'You *are* getting better, aren't you? Wait until I tell you what's been going on in the village.'

'Let me tell you something first,' said Rosa. 'I had another bad dream.'

'Probably because you were feverish.'

'Perhaps, but it woke me up . . . and something made me look out of the window.'

'And?'

'Someone was having a bonfire down on the meadow – near the washing-machine, I think.'

'Really?' said Tom thoughtfully. 'It may have been someone dumping rubbish. Let's hope they used that mouldy sock to light it. I think something must have been going on at the post office last night as well. There was a police car outside and only Sharee was serving in the shop. She wouldn't say what was going on and when I asked to see Jamie about tea she said I'd best call back later.'

They heard the telephone ringing in the hall. This was rare in Hetty's house because, although she had owned a telephone for years, it was understood that it was only to be used for occasional long-distance calls or emergencies. After a few minutes Hetty came into Rosa's bedroom.

'That was Jamie,' she said. 'He says he can't manage tea today and could you make it for lunch tomorrow instead.'

'That's probably just as well with Rosa ill,' said Tom. 'I wouldn't mind knowing what's been going on, though.'

'I should keep well away for the moment,' said Hetty. 'He said he'd explain everything when he saw you.' She had obviously heard about the police car. 'If you want something to do you can help me clean the windows. They're rather grubby after that rainstorm. Why don't you go and get the bucket and leather while I settle your sister down.'

She turned the bolster and straigtened the sheets before speaking.

'You would tell me if anything was worrying you, wouldn't you, dear?' she said. 'It's so unlike you to be ill. Of course you had the chickenpox and all those things when you were younger, but you weren't one for bugs. I'm wondering if I ought to ring your mother. I would have rung her this morning but I know she's busy with the summer conference, so I decided to see if you perked up a bit during the day.'

'There's really no need to tell Mum,' said Rosa. 'I feel so much better now.'

'You haven't answered my question,' said Hetty.

'I did have a nightmare,' said Rosa. 'I think that made me very tired.'

'Yes?'

Hetty waited.

'And we had a bit of an argument with Jake Florey.'

'Whenever did you meet *him*?'

'We had a walk the day before yesterday. It was on a right of way but he wasn't very happy about us being there.'

'Take my advice, girl, and keep right away from those Floreys, right of way or not.'

While Hetty fetched more balm tea Rosa had another look out of her window. She was reassured to see that Jake was not at his look-out post.

TEN

Lunch with Jamie was an informal affair.

'Mum has to stay in the shop so we'll have to fend for ourselves,' he said. 'It's one of our busiest times, and Dad rarely comes home midday.'

'Where does he work?' asked Rosa.

'Down at Pineways Furniture Warehouse in Sladbury. It was much better when they both worked here, but it just didn't bring in enough money. Dad helps with a few of the lifting jobs here and Sharee comes in a few hours a week, otherwise it's just Mum.'

They were in the flat above the shop, in a large square room that was used for sitting and eating. Tom and Rosa sat on a sagging brown sofa. The low table in front of them was littered with folders and sheets of figures, as was the dining-table by the wall. The sideboard was cluttered with dusty china figures, an unhealthy fern, piles of old newspapers and a huge basket of ironing.

Jamie prepared lunch. A small kitchen was separated from the main part of the room by a formica-topped breakfast bar. The counters were untidy with cereal boxes, sticky jars of marmalade, the peel of half a grapefruit and piles of dirty breakfast plates.

'Sorry about the mess,' said Jamie. 'We're having a hectic time at the moment. I suppose you heard about the break-in?' He held up a tin of spaghetti dinosaurs. 'Hope this is all right. Mum started buying them when I was three years old and never got out of the habit.' He opened the tin and slopped the orange contents into a pan. The end of the plastic pan handle had melted into a black blob.

'What break-in?' said Tom, trying not to sound too interested.

'The one here,' said Jamie. 'They climbed into the back-yard and broke into the stock room.'

'What did they nick?'

'Surprisingly little really; a few sweets and cigarettes, that's all. They didn't bother with the shop apart from tipping a few things on to the floor. The biggest problem was the mess they made in the back room. They emptied the filing cabinet, tore up heaps of important papers and poured Coke all over them. Some records are missing completely. They're probably in a bin somewhere. There's usually someone in the house, but we were out at my Aunt Molly's till late. It made us feel as though they'd been watching the flat, waiting for us to leave.'

'What did the police say?' asked Rosa.

'They reckon it was kids and that they didn't bother with the shop in case they were seen from the road. I said they must have had pretty good tools to deal with the locks and bolts on that door. I told them we thought it was like Fort Knox — more like Opportunity Knocks they said. They asked Mum all sorts of questions; she spent most of the time sobbing and saying that she wouldn't rest easy in her bed. They tried to cheer her up by telling her the Crime Prevention Officer would advise her on how to make the place more secure in future.'

'I think they're right about the Crime Prevention Officer,' said Rosa seriously. 'Mum got them in last year after we'd had a lot of local break-ins. They showed her how easy it is to get in through ordinary windows and doors. She spent a fortune on a special front door lock and had all the windows done, but she reckoned it was worth it for the peace of mind.'

'I suppose you're right,' said Jamie. 'I'll have a word with Mum when she's calmed down a bit, but I don't expect we can afford it.'

He took several slices of bread from a plastic packet and put them in the toaster.

'Tell me if you see smoke,' he said. 'This toaster has a mind of its own.'

'I'll come and watch it,' said Tom.

'You could clean up some plates, too,' said Jamie, 'if you can find the sink.'

Rosa still felt drowsy. A large goldfish goggled at her from a bowl which stood behind the dead fern on the sideboard. The bowl was slimy with filth and the only relief for the fish from the boredom of swimming in small circles was a tiny arch which was clearly too small for it to get through.

'Like her?' said Jamie. 'She's called Boadicea. She had a mate called Caesar, but he got stuck in the arch and snuffed it. She's never got over the shock. Keeps searching for him . . . even outside the bowl. My dad had to kip on the sofa when my aunt came to stay and woke up to find the fish had leapt out of the bowl on to his face. She slipped down inside the sleeping-bag, the zip got stuck and we found Dad leaping about the room yelling that there was a fish in his pyjamas. We only just found her in time!'

'Do you mind if I bring her a new tank?' said Rosa, laughing. 'The poor thing is far too cramped in there. Hetty's got a tank we used for stick insects one year. I'm sure she wouldn't mind you having it.'

'In case you haven't noticed,' said Tom, 'Rosa is a great animal lover. Not that I'm knocking it. You should have seen her with Jake Florey's dogs.'

Rosa gave Tom a warning look. 'Any chance of some food?' she said. 'I'm starving.'

They ate their spaghetti on toast, followed by cups of tea and Mars Bars. Then, after a half-hearted attempt at clearing up, they watched a video recording of 'Top of the Pops'.

'I shall have to go after this,' said Jamie. 'I promised Mum I'd help with the stock. But, listen, I'm going to Wescombe with her and my aunt tomorrow. We go from Sladbury by coach. Fancy coming? I could use a bit of company.'

ELEVEN

As Pineways was open on Sundays, Mr Hopkins dropped them off at the coach station on his way to work. Although they were quite early the Wescombe coach was crowded. Rosa, Tom and Jamie shared a double seat near the back, leaving a seat at the front for Mrs Hopkins and Jamie's Aunt Molly.

'I'm sure the children can do without us oldies to talk to, bless 'em,' said Mrs Hopkins as she squeezed into the seat beside her equally large sister. 'I do hope they remembered to spend a penny.'

'They're quite big enough to look after themselves now,' said Molly. She took out a bag of fudge cubes and popped a piece into her mouth. 'And don't expect them to tag along with us all day.'

The coach was stuffy from stale ash, exhaust fumes and standing in the sun. As they juddered out on to the road Rosa pulled down the air nozzle to try and freshen the air.

'Don't expect much conversation out of Rosa,' said Tom. 'She gets travel sick.'

Jamie produced a packet of extra strong mints from his Supersports bag. 'Suck one of these,' he said. 'Aunt Molly swears by them.'

Rosa shook her head.

'She won't,' said Tom. 'She's got no fillings.'

'I'm a lost cause,' said Jamie cheerfully. 'I've got more filling than tooth.'

He produced Bold Wars, an electronic space game, which kept him and Tom amused for a while. Rosa tried to watch but it made her sick to stare at the tiny screen. Instead, she looked out of the window and tried to anticipate the curves in the road.

As they got near to the coast the clouds thickened and large drops of rain fell on the dusty windows.

'I don't think we'll get much sun,' said Rosa.

'Never mind,' said Jamie. 'There's loads to do on the pier. I hope you've brought some cash.'

It was pouring by the time they arrived at Wescombe. The roads were crowded with mackintoshed tourists, moving from one stuffy amusement arcade to another. Those who had no rainwear protected their heads with towels, bags and even beachballs, but a man selling Super Ted balloons stood on a corner bare-headed and smiled as if it were the finest day of summer. Polystyrene chip plates and grease floated on pools of water that had collected in blocked gutters and the paper on the news hoardings was so wet that yesterday's news showed through.

The coach stopped along the sea front, near the pier.

'Cooee, Jamie!' called Mrs Hopkins, flapping a newspaper above her head in case he hadn't noticed her. 'We're going on the pier. It's raining buckets so we'll make a dash for it. Are you coming with us?'

There was a central partition down the pier. On either side of it, beneath a small roof, were wooden benches. One side received the full force of the weather, but on the other a few pensioners sat in their raincoats, determined to keep their favourite seats in case it got fine again. There wasn't much for them to see; apart from a huddle of donkeys under the pier the beach was empty.

Tom, Rosa and Jamie followed the two ladies down the pier. They tried to keep in the shelter of the central partition but by the time they reached the amusement arcade they were drenched. (Although Mrs Hopkins' wiry hair seemed remarkably unaffected by the soaking.)

'We're gasping for a coffee,' said Molly, shaking the drops off a plastic rainhat. 'You coming in the caff?'

They peered into the poky café. Every plastic seat was taken and there was a blue haze of cigarette smoke.

'Let's not,' said Rosa. 'The smoke makes me feel sick.'

The children looked round the arcade. Jamie was keen on the one-armed bandits and Space Invaders and got quite excited when Rosa soon won some tokens on Quids In.

'I don't want to feed them back into these,' she said. 'I'll have a look round and meet you by the House of Horrors in ten minutes.'

She couldn't find much to interest her until a small boy tugged her arm. ''Ave a look at this,' he said. He pointed to a game called Super Crane, in which a crane-like claw hovered over a tub of small prizes.

'It's me last token,' he said, pushing it into the slot, 'and I'm feelin' lucky.' The machine clicked and whirred and the boy pressed his dirty face up against the glass to watch. The claw jerked over the dusty objects and closed around a green plastic dinosaur.

'Got it!' he said.

But the dinosaur fell out of the claw and the boy let out a stream of bad language.

'Bad luck,' said Rosa.

The boy shrugged. 'You 'aving a go?' he said.

'Leave the lass alone,' said a man. He stood with his back to them, intent upon the game he was playing.

'That's me dad,' said the boy. ''E's 'aving a go on Holocaust.'

'We'd better have another go on this, then,' said Rosa. 'And if we win anything you can have it . . . if your dad says it's all right.'

'He can 'ave what 'e likes as long as it keeps 'im quiet,' said the man without turning.

They had no luck with the first token, but with the second the claw closed swiftly round a plastic egg, swung around and dropped the prize down a metal chute.

'There you are,' said Rosa.

The boy snatched it without thanks and split the egg open to reveal some pink sweets and a slip of paper.

'Don't want the motto,' he said. He dropped it on to the floor, where it lodged between two boards. Rosa could see the glint of the sea below and it was tempting to let it float down into the water.

But she picked it up.

'What's it say, then?' said the boy. His cheeks were bulging with sweets and a drop of sugary pink saliva dribbled on to his chin.

'It's pathetic,' said Rosa. She screwed up the paper and thrust it deep into her pocket.

*

Tom was waiting at the House of Horrors.

'Jamie's gone in,' said Tom. 'He says his mum's always calling him a horror and he'd like to see why.'

'I'm glad he's not here,' said Rosa grimly. 'I need to talk.'

'What's up?' said Tom.

'This,' she said.

She handed him the screw of paper. He opened it up. It read:

R. H. see Ivy Wothers today.

It was written in spidery, old-fashioned writing.

'Who gave you this?' asked Tom. 'We don't know an Ivy Wothers.'

'I won it in a machine – that one with the crane that picks up prizes. It was inside a plastic egg.'

'What did you have a go on that for? It's rubbish.'

'I was trying to win something for a little boy.'

'This must be an advertisement for Ivy Whatsit. She'll be in the arcade running a bingo stall or something.'

'But it's handwritten, Tom, and it says R.H., my initials.'

'That's a bit strange, but I'm sure it's only a coincidence. It probably stands for "Ruined Holiday" or "Rotten Hoax".'

'I suppose so,' said Rosa. 'But it makes me feel uneasy.'

They left the pier at lunchtime to find the nearest fish restaurant. The place smelt of burnt cooking fat and damp clothing, but seemed fairly clean. They collected their haddock and chips and sat on hard plastic seats at a red formica table. Molly pushed a forkful of chips into her mouth and peered out through the steamy window.

'That wind's a blessing in disguise,' she said. 'I do believe it's blowing the clouds away.'

It was true. There were already quite large patches of blue sky.

'It'll be on to the beach for me once I've bought a souvenir,' she said, putting a large piece of fish in her mouth.

'Aunt Molly likes to collect souvenirs of all her trips,' explained Jamie. 'She's got a shelf full of them.'

'It's my little hobby,' said Molly, pink with pleasure at the interest she was receiving. 'And I've seen some little plates with a picture of Wescombe in the middle that would look really nice with the jug I got last time. Mind you, I mustn't spend too much today. I'm not a working woman any more . . .'

A tear rolled down her cheek and made an orange channel in her face powder.

'We were really sorry to hear about your job,' said Rosa gently.

Tom gave her an anxious look. He didn't want her to upset Molly.

'It's nice of you to say so, dear,' said Molly, 'but you'll not find me feeling sorry for myself.' She sniffed and bit into an enormous chip butty. 'I'm not one to wallow in self-pity. And it's not as if *I* was in the wrong. That Florey has a lot to answer for.'

'Quite so,' said Jamie. 'Good for you, Aunty. Want the rest of my chips? I'm full.'

By the time they got to the beach the sky was clear, but there was still a strong wind. Wescombe was an estuary resort and the tide was going out to leave a strip of muddy sand. It wasn't swimsuit weather, but several deckchairs had been erected and most people had at least kicked off their shoes. A toddler marched proudly up the beach with a bucket full of sticky brown water; his track-suit bottoms were rolled up to reveal mud stains up to his ankles.

'Let's have a deckchair, Molly,' said Mrs Hopkins. 'I'm too old for sitting on sand. My treat.' She gave Jamie the money and sent him off. 'You going on the donkeys?' she asked Tom.

'Leave off, Betty,' laughed Molly. 'He's a young man now. What would he be wanting with donkey rides?'

The donkeys plodded patiently across the beach, their hooves kicking up clods of wet sand.

'We'll probably have a walk along the front,' said Tom politely. 'Shall we meet at four-thirty at the coach stop?'

The three children walked so far along the front that they nearly rounded the point into the next bay. The wind roared in their ears, dried their lips and faces, and made the corners of their eyes tingle. Breathless, they sat on a bench to watch the beach. A cigarette carton cartwheeled by, and above it a huge kite dipped and soared, flaunting its magnificent dragon face and multicoloured tail. Youngsters bounced on a large inflatable castle, squealing as they fell. The sea, flat and grey, was so far out that it could not be heard.

It was as they were walking back towards the main shopping centre that Rosa noticed the woman. She was small, old and dressed in black and looked so out of place with her long woollen coat and neat little hat that Rosa was surprised that nobody else seemed to be watching her. She walked towards them along the front with her smart black shoes clicking and in her hand she carried a large black bag. She moved quickly and kept her head well down as she passed them, but there was time for Rosa to see the initials on the bag. Printed in gold beneath the lock were the letters I. W.

'See that?' she whispered to Tom.

He looked puzzled.

'I. W.,' she said. 'Does that remind you of anything?'

'Absolutely nothing,' he said.

'Ivy Wothers,' she said. 'Remember my note? I'm going back. You keep with Jamie. I'll see you outside the ice-cream shop by the pier.'

And she was gone, rushing along the front as though she had an important appointment to keep.

'Where's she off to?' said Jamie.

As Tom was not sure he said nothing.

It was hard to keep up with the woman, but Rosa was glad as it gave her a moment to decide how she was going to introduce herself to a perfect stranger.

Further along the front the woman crossed the road. She stopped in a sheltered alcove in the brick wall that ran beside the crazy-golf course and began to take something from her black bag. At first it looked like the wooden frame of a kite, but as she opened it out it grew and Rosa could see stripy cloth like a small parachute. With a bit of adjustment here and there the woman tidied it up to form a neat tent. She pulled two canvas-seated stools from the bag, opened them up and placed them in the tent, hung a printed sign by the door, and went inside.

Rosa crossed the road. The sign said:

IVY WOTHERS
Granddaughter of Neptune the Magnificent
FORTUNES TOLD
STEP INSIDE

So Rosa stepped inside.

The tent was small and the canvas stool uncomfortable, but it was good to get out of the wind. Ivy Wothers was tiny and frail, with pale skin like crinkled tissue paper. She had a grannyish quality that made Rosa relax a little.

'Are you Rosa?' she said.

Rosa had expected her to sound more confident.

'Yes. I had your message.'

'Clever girl. Not many would take it seriously and my powers are not what they were. You're very young, but suitable.'

'Suitable for what?'

'I'm here to tell you about The Gift. We may never meet again, so listen carefully.'

The woman looked around anxiously as the canvas flapped in the wind.

'I hope you're being honest with me. You are Rosa, aren't you? It's been thirty years since someone suitable had it and my strength has been sapped by waiting. Try to understand me.'

The woman stopped speaking and closed her eyes; her head drooped down on to her chest as if she had fallen asleep.

'Are you all right?' said Rosa anxiously.

The woman sat up, startled.

'I'm weary, that's all.'

'Shouldn't you go home?'

'I can't rest yet.

' "Guard it, little Ivy," he said. "It will have no power for you. Neptune's granddaughter has no need of it. It is with a worthy person. She must bring it to you when she no longer has need of it. Guard it for her, Ivy, and pass it on when the time is right. But take care . . . It must not get into the wrong hands. Do this twice, Ivy, then I shall appoint another." I should never have promised him. I knew my limitations. I managed once, but then I let him down . . . and Violet too.'

'What do you need to tell me?' asked Rosa.

The tent was beginning to feel very hot.

'I have to put things right, Rosa.'

'What things?'

'Seek it in Nettlesfield. I passed it to the wrong person.

54

It wasn't safe with her. It's in safe hands now, but she doesn't understand the dangers. I'd have got it myself but I never leave Wescombe. *"Give it to the newborn when she's ready,"* I said.'

She stopped to get her breath.

'Don't trust the wrong person or someone will be in danger . . . don't let anyone get there first or it's lost again. Ask the right person and she'll know what to do . . . Violet told me to give it to Connie. I got it wrong. I was ill and muddled.'

'Connie? She was my grandma.'

'I have to believe you,' she said. 'It's in good hands now . . . but the secret's out again. Only you can save The Gift.'

The woman stood, folded up her stool and began to put it into the black bag.

'I don't understand,' said Rosa. She was beginning to feel puzzled, frightened.

'I'm getting weaker,' said Ivy.

She began to dismantle the tent. She packed it into her bag along with her stool and gestured for Rosa to hand her the remaining stool.

'How can I save this Gift thing if you don't tell me who's got it?'

'I wish I dared say,' said Ivy. 'But I was caught that way before. You might have been sent.'

She began to walk away.

'Where do I start? I don't even know what The Gift is.'

Ivy paused for a moment before walking round the corner.

'There'll be ashes . . . the ashes,' she said. 'You'll get help from an unexpected source.'

Her voice was so quiet it was hard to hear.

*

Rosa woke to find faces peering at her. Only she wasn't in Aunt Hetty's back bedroom this time. She could taste salt in the air.

'She's fainted, she 'as,' said a woman unnecessarily.

'Summer flu,' said another. 'There's a lot of it about.'

Someone felt her forehead with an icy hand.

'She's feverish.'

'Ooh look, she's opening 'er eyes. We'd best find out who she is.'

'It's all right,' said a calm voice. 'She's my sister. I can deal with the matter now, thank you.'

The women stayed where they were.

'I'm sure it would help my sister if she had a little more space,' said Tom.

The women left reluctantly.

'What was 'e doing letting 'er out with a fever I'd like to know,' said one of them.

Tom and Jamie sat Rosa up.

'Head down,' said Tom. 'And take deep breaths.'

'Good job we walked back to meet you,' said Jamie. 'Those women might have tried first aid on you.'

Later they walked back to the coach stop. Tom made Rosa sit on a bench and Jamie bought her a huge ice-cream.

'Eat this,' he said. 'It'll cure anything.'

A herring gull tussled with a greasy bag in the gutter and soared away with a chip in its beak. Rosa could see Molly and Mrs Hopkins approaching, laden with shopping bags.

'Don't tell them about me feeling dizzy, will you?' she said to the boys. 'I don't want to spoil the day for them.'

As Jamie walked up to meet them, Tom said: 'It wasn't just a case of feeling dizzy, was it?'

'No,' said Rosa. 'It was much more than that.'

TWELVE

om and Rosa did not discuss things until the following
morning. They went to Berry Mill in Farnsworth. It
was only a bus drive and short walk away and had always
been special for them. In the past it had been used to
finish the cloth woven in the little cottages on the hill
but it had been derelict for years. Tom and Rosa had a
secret entrance and knew they would be able to talk
there.

But things had changed. In the yard by the mill stood
a small caravan and a rusting Morris Minor. Beside them
were piles of sand and cement, an old wheelbarrow and
an encrusted cement-mixer. A line of washing hung from
an old hook on the mill wall and beneath a green

tarpaulin stood a neat stack of Cotswold stone. A woman in overalls came out of the caravan; she walked over to the mixer and shovelled in some sand.

'Hello there,' she said, pushing her long hair off her face.

'Is it all right if we come through?' asked Tom.

'Sure,' she said. 'We may have bought the place but we don't intend to stop people from using the old path. We hope they'll spend a bit of money here when we've opened up.'

'What are you doing with it?' asked Rosa.

'We're going to do dressmaking and knitting in one end,' she said, 'and live in the other. We may sell teas in the bit overlooking the mill wheel.'

They heard squeals of delight from the lakeside. Two girls stood on the edge throwing in bread scraps from a brown paper bag. The lake was filled by a stream that ran from the trout farm up the valley and eager fish darted up to gobble the crumbs the moment they touched the surface.

'Don't let Angharad get too close,' called the woman, peering anxiously round the corner.

'Don't worry, Mummy,' said the older child.

One path ran alongside the water and the other up the wooded hillside. Tom and Rosa took the latter. The wood was noisy with birds and the ground was a tangle of creepers and tiny flowers. They sat on a fallen tree trunk; insects scurried along the routeways in the crusty bark.

'I never thought anybody would take Berry Mill on,' said Tom. 'It always seemed too far gone.'

'Why can't things stay the same?' said Rosa unhappily.

'Nothing seems the same this holiday,' said Tom. 'That's why we need to talk.'

Rosa nodded.

'We've had trouble with Jake and his father, and Jamie's place has been wrecked,' she said. 'It just doesn't feel so comfortable at Hetty's any more.'

'But that's not all, is it?' said Tom.

Rosa wore a stubborn expression; he would have to choose his words carefully.

'It's you I'm worried about.'

'Don't bother,' said Rosa. 'I'll be fine.'

'Not if you go fainting all over the place,' said Tom. 'You may not have anybody with you next time. And what about the bad dreams; I found you sleepwalking, remember?'

Rosa stood. Her shoulders were hunched and stiff as if she were about to cry.

'Talk to me about it, Rosa,' said Tom. 'I may be able to help.'

She sat again and folded her arms tightly together. 'I've been having the strangest feelings since we came to Hetty's,' she said. Her voice was almost a whisper. 'It's as though something takes me over – eggs me on to do things that I'd never dare – like Jake Florey's labradors. I love animals, but I must have been a fool to hold out my arms to attacking dogs.'

'*And* you tackled Giles Florey,' said Tom.

Rosa stared down through the trees.

'Yesterday was the oddest of all,' she said softly. 'I met Ivy Wothers. She *was* a fortune-teller and she was expecting me.'

'They're usually a big con,' said Tom.

'I know. Her sign said she was the granddaughter of Neptune the Magnificent. It sounded so daft I thought she *must* be a fraud . . . and yet she knew a few things that convinced me she was genuine.'

'Can you remember what she said?' asked Tom.

'Most of it, but I don't understand it. She seemed very

59

anxious and spoke in riddles. First she told me I was *suitable* . . . that was because I'd found her message. Then she said she must tell me about The Gift . . .'

'What gift?'

'Goodness knows. She said it had been thirty years since someone suitable had it. She'd given it to the wrong person but it was in safe hands now. She told me the secret was out again and I was the only one who could save it.'

'It must be an advertising gimmick: collect your free gift and be plagued with catalogues for the rest of your life.'

'I thought it must be a trick at first, but she knew about Nettlesfield and said I should look for it there.'

'She could have heard us talking.'

'Not about Grandma Connie. She said Violet had told her to give it to Connie but she'd got it wrong.'

'Did she say anything else?'

'Nothing that made much sense. I was starting to feel dizzy. She wouldn't tell me what The Gift was *or* who had got it. It was as if she didn't believe it was really me. She even suggested I might have been sent.'

'Where was she?'

'Don't you remember? I followed her along the front.'

Tom looked puzzled. He had not seen her.

'She put up her tent where you found me,' said Rosa. 'You must only just have missed her.'

'Pity,' said Tom. 'I wouldn't have minded listening in on your little chat.'

'I think we should ask Hetty if she's heard of someone called Violet,' said Rosa.

'She told you to look for this Gift in Nettlesfield . . . but where? Didn't she give you any other clues?'

'No,' said Rosa, 'but I'm scared that if I don't find it something awful is going to happen.'

'Do you think your dreams could be part of it?'

'I'm not even sure the first one *was* a dream. It was about tapping in the loft, but I was out of bed and I saw a loft ladder. It was so *real*.'

'You must have dreamed it. There is no loft ladder.'

'How do you know?'

'I sort of brought it into conversation with Hetty by asking her if she had any more photos up there. She said no one had been up there for years, probably because they couldn't be bothered to get the ladder up from the shed.'

'So you took my dreams seriously?'

'I've never seen anything shake you up like that before,' he said grimly. 'What about the second dream?'

'I was *in* the loft . . . there was an old typewriter on a table and I was frightened.'

'A typewriter? I wonder if that had anything to do with the tapping noise. Was there anything else?'

'Yes. There was someone there, someone who looked like Hetty.'

'But what frightened you?'

'The creaking, I think. I could hear a creaking noise . . . and it scared me.'

'What about the dream you had before you were ill? Was that in the loft?'

'Yes. A man was coming. He said, "Where is it, woman?" I knew I had to hide something from him, but I wasn't sure what to do.'

'Did you see the man?'

'No, but I was waiting for him . . . I knew he was coming.'

'Was he looking for what you're looking for now?'

Beads of perspiration stood out on Rosa's forehead.

'I don't know.'

'Never mind. We'll find out.'

'How?'

Tom was flattered to be asked. Rosa usually had clear plans of her own.

'First we ask Hetty about Violet.'

'And then?'

'We go in the loft, of course.'

They walked up the wood path to the tiny grey cottages. A fat black cat with yellow eyes sat on a wall, with a money spider swaying up and down from its whiskers. Some stone steps led down between two cottages to join the lake path. By the time they walked round to the mill the children had gone. A bit of bread that the trout had missed lay soggily on the water.

'Do you kids want to see the wheel moving?' called a man from the yard. He climbed over to a platform above the mill wheel and removed a snail-covered plank. Weed hung from it like a green beard.

'It's working,' said Rosa excitedly. 'Let's get closer.'

As they watched neat drops sprayed out from the wheel and were suspended in the air for a moment like strings of diamonds.

THIRTEEN

For supper Hetty made baked eggs in tomatoes with basil. Tom sat at the table to watch as she scooped out the centres of the sweet tomatoes with a spoon. She mixed basil, chives, salt and pepper into the tomato pulp, adding wholemeal breadcrumbs to make a thick paste, and then counted six brown eggs from a china bowl on the dresser.

'Fresh laid this morning,' she said. 'I got them from Betty at the hairdresser's.' She cradled each egg in her hand for a moment before breaking it into a hollowed tomato, then covered each one with breadcrumb mixture before deftly sliding it into an oval earthenware dish. She put the dish in the Aga and the heat from the oven made her face go pink.

They ate the eggs forty minutes later with crusty wholemeal rolls, and finished with fresh fruit salad and cream.

Afterwards they all read. Rosa was finishing a novel and Hetty read the newspaper. Tom picked the dictionary off the shelf and browsed through it. He turned to the section of names at the back.

'I like looking through the names, don't you?' he said. 'I bet you haven't heard this one – "Aluin, friend of all" – and what about Basil? We had him for supper!'

Neither of the others reacted.

'Listen, Rosa,' he said. 'I'm going to find several names that come from plants, like yours. Imagine being called Cherry or Daisy.'

'I know a Hazel,' said Rosa, realizing what Tom was doing. 'What about you, Hetty?'

'There's an Iris who works at the library,' she said. 'And our mother was friendly with Violet Bishop.'

'Dotty Dora's mother?'

'Yes, though you mustn't call her that.'

'Sorry,' said Tom, 'but she is a bit odd.'

'She was always a simple soul, but she took on worse when our Connie died. Connie was so good with her; she was only eleven when Dora was born but she dealt with her like a mother.'

'Dora must have missed Connie when she got married.'

'She did, poor girl, but whenever Connie visited from Hampton Leonard she'd be sure to drop in to see Dora and bring her a treat.'

'Did Violet like Connie?' said Rosa.

'Yes, she had a real soft spot for her. She liked the way Connie dealt with Dora – kind without being condescending. She said Connie had a real way with her, a gift.'

'When did Violet die?'

'A long while back. Must have been 1958, two years before my mother. But Dora wasn't alone. She still had her father, Albert. He lived on for another sixteen years or so.' Hetty folded up her newspaper. 'And now, if you'll excuse me, I'm going up to bed. I suddenly feel rather tired.'

'I wonder why she doesn't want to talk about it?' said Tom.

Tom was acting strangely at breakfast the following morning. He yawned loudly and Rosa thought he had ruffled his hair deliberately.

'Had a bad night?' said Hetty as she popped his toasted rye bread on a pretty china plate.

'I'm afraid you've got a bit of a problem, Hetty,' he said. 'I think there's a visitor in the loft. There was something rustling about above my room. Do birds ever get stuck in there?'

'I have had trouble with starlings, but not usually at this time of year. One got into the loft a few years ago; it squeezed down beside the water pipes into the airing cupboard. I found it sitting on my best linen and quite a mess it had made of it, too, with feathers and droppings. I tried to pick it up but it flew out into the cottage.'

'How did you get the poor thing out?' said Rosa.

'I opened as many windows as I could and eventually shooed it out of one. Then I had Rod Johnson in to fill all the gaps in the eaves so it wouldn't happen again. It must have been a couple of years back so I suppose they could have found a way in. I'll call and ask Rod to pop round. I've got to go past his house this morning.'

'I'll take a look at it if you like,' said Tom. 'I think I know what to do. We had a bird in our roof once, didn't we, Rosa? How do you get up there?'

'The only ladder that will reach is that rickety wooden one in the shed. Do be careful if you use that.'

'I will,' said Tom. 'Rosa will help me, won't you?'

She nodded.

Tom smiled to himself. 'Got any more of that rye bread, Hetty?' he said.

The garden shed was cluttered with the sort of things that might come in handy one day. There were half-used tins of paint with dribbles down their sides like candle wax, old baskets, a rusty bicycle wheel, a bag of cat litter and numerous cardboard boxes of tools and tins. The ladder, of course, was at the back. It was ancient; its steps were blobbed with various colours of paint and the hinges on the top were loose.

'If we tighten the screws a bit it will be fine,' said Tom. 'See if there's a screwdriver in one of the boxes, would you, and I'll collect a few convincing tools.'

'Do you think she suspected anything?' said Rosa.

'With my acting? Never!'

'It's all a bit sneaky, Tom. I'm not really happy about it.'

'You will be happy if it solves the mystery. We know who Violet was now – Dora's mum. Ivy Wothers said something about Violet wanting her to give it to Connie. Our grandma was meant to have The Gift, but Ivy gave it to the wrong person.'

'The wrong person could be anybody.'

'Not really. It would have to be someone Violet knew and someone Ivy could mistake for Connie.'

'Hetty?'

'Possibly. She might have meant to give something to Connie and got the wrong sister.'

'But she said it wasn't safe with her. I can't imagine something being unsafe with Hetty.'

'It depends what this Gift is. Let's hope there are some clues in the loft.'

The loft was long and low. It had a skylight at the back but Hetty said that if they were going to find a bird they would also need their torches.

'Well,' said Tom, after they had both hauled themselves up. 'Is this the loft in your dreams?'

'It looks the same,' said Rosa. 'But it doesn't feel the same.'

'It might have done years ago. Look at all these boxes. Hetty seems to be quite well organized. They've all got luggage labels on them.'

They read the labels: 'Pots and pans', 'Spare sheets', 'Shoes'. There were two old kitchen chairs, a lamp stand and a sledge with rusty runners, bundles of old books and pictures and a dusty old mirror.

'Does any of this lot mean anything to you?' said Tom.

'No,' said Rosa. 'It just looks like a typical loft to me.'

'There's certainly no sign of the table and typewriter.'

'Or any evidence that there was ever a loft ladder fixed by the trap door.'

They heard Hetty's voice below.

'Just coming, Hetty,' called Tom. 'There's no bird here now, but I think I've found the hole. It's just a tile out of place. We'll be down in a moment.'

Before she left, Rosa looked out of the skylight. She could just make out the shape of Nettlebury Manor across the hazy fields.

FOURTEEN

Rosa was dreaming.

'Try to remember . . . Try to remember . . .'
'Who is it?'
'We met.'
'Who are you?'
'We met. Remember my last words. Follow the clues.'
It was Ivy Wothers.
'Tell me again.'
'I have not the strength . . .'
'Don't go. Come back!'

Tom was there by her bed.

'You've had another one, haven't you? You were yelling in your sleep. What happened?'

Rosa sat up. She felt hot. Confused.

'It was Ivy. But I couldn't see her. She seemed weak . . . said I should remember her last words and follow the clues.'

'It must mean something she said at Wescombe. You must have been trying to remember it in your dream.'

'It felt as though she was really trying to reach me. She wants me to remember her last words.'

'Think it through,' urged Tom.

'I remember her putting up the tent. We went in and she talked about my being "suitable". She was there to tell me about The Gift. It had been thirty years since someone suitable had it. Violet had wanted Connie to have it but she had got it wrong.'

'What else?'

'I can't remember.'

'There was that thing about it being in good hands now but you had to get there quickly.'

'I'm not even sure she said that. I was starting to feel hot. She began to pack up her stool and take down the tent. Everything was going black.'

'What did she say as she left? Was there anything else?'

'Yes, I asked how I could save The Gift if she wouldn't tell me what it was. That was when she said I might have been sent. But I've told you that before.'

'Was that the last thing she said?'

'No. I called after her again. My voice sounded hollow . . . I was falling . . . but I heard something as I went down . . . "There'll be ashes . . . the ashes. You'll get help from an unexpected source."'

'That's it!' said Tom. 'Her last words. We've got to look in the ashes. She must mean the fire you saw the other night.'

Rosa did not relish the thought of going on the Floreys' land again, but she was too tired to argue.

FIFTEEN

There was no sign of Dora Bishop or her dog as they went down beside her garden to the copse. The squirrel was there and Rosa had collected a pocket full of nuts, but she could only persuade the chattering creature on to her hand by sending Tom on ahead.

Tom crossed the little bridge and walked past the washing-machine and three willows to the spot where they had met Jake. He felt a bit nervous and was relieved to see Rosa emerging from the copse behind him. A little way up the meadow he discovered a dark round where the fire had been. It had been thoroughly burned and well raked over. He pushed a stick into the centre. Flakes of white ash floated up and stuck to his trousers. There was nothing to find there.

'There's nothing in the ashes,' he called, 'but there are fresh tyre tracks here. Florey could easily have driven across the fields. There'd only be a few gates to open.'

Rosa had crossed the bridge and was peering into the reeds near the willows.

'Have a look at this,' she said. 'An empty petrol can. Whoever burned that fire wanted to make sure it went up well. We're not going to find any clues here. Let's go, Tom. The Floreys might turn up any minute.'

'I'll have a last look round and catch you up,' he said.

It was when he walked beside the river towards the bridge that he noticed the paper; a small wodge of it, brittle from the fire, was stuck in the reeds. The outer sheets flaked away as he picked it up but a few pieces in the centre remained intact. They were of lined paper, like a notebook, and there was writing on them. He found an empty crisp bag in his pocket and carefully slid the delicate layers inside it.

As he stepped on to the bridge he had an uneasy feeling that he was being watched. He turned in time to see a flash of light from an upstairs window in Nettlebury Manor.

Later they spread newspaper on the floor of Tom's room, cut open the crisp bag with a pair of nail scissors and, with the aid of a sharp knife from the kitchen drawer, began to separate the delicate flakes of paper. It was frustrating; most of the paper was so thin that it crumbled into a black mess. But one piece in the centre held together. It was singed rather than burned and the writing was legible.

'It looks pretty old-fashioned, like Hetty's handwriting,' said Rosa.

'Let's copy it down in case it crumbles,' said Tom.
It showed parts of two entries in a diary.

> . . . *my dogs on Stinchampton Common. I met Jimmy Barnett and took the opportunity to ask him to deal with vermin in the barn* . . .
> . . . *wasted on that crone. What's the harm if I relieve her of it and put it to good use. If she's telling the truth I'll have it and if she is lying* . . .

'Do you think it's to do with The Gift?' said Tom.
'I doubt it. If it is why burn it there? Anyone in Gozzards Reach or up on the common could see it.'
'Perhaps someone was meant to see it,' said Tom.

Jamie called at Tanglewild that afternoon. Hetty was out at Lotty Carpenter's.
'Can we talk?' he said. 'I've got something that might interest you.'
They went up to Tom's room.
'I've got this friend at school,' he began. 'She's called Yan Yan. She rang the other day to say they were back from abroad. Their flight didn't get them in until late Thursday evening so they were driving over Stinchampton Common just after 1 a.m. on Friday. She wanted to know if there had been a bonfire party by the river because she'd noticed a fire down in Florey's meadow.'
Rosa and Tom exchanged looks.
'I didn't think much of it at the time, what with having the break-in and Mum crying all over the place. But later I couldn't help feeling suspicious. We'd had that row with Florey that day and I wouldn't put it past him to have sent some heavies round to wreck the place.'
Tom nodded.
'And what better to do with the nicked papers than

burn them? It would be just like him to think he couldn't be seen at night.'

'Did you tell the police?' asked Tom.

'I did better than that. I went to look in the ashes last evening. I thought I'd tell the law if I found anything.'

'Did you find anything?'

'Not from the shop, but there was something that might interest you. There was nothing in the ashes, but I found a few sheets of burned paper that had blown up the meadow. They were pretty far gone, but I could read one bit. I've got it here.' He carefully slid an envelope out of one of his pockets and eased out the charred paper.

They read:

> . . . giving up the search as the assault on the cottage was a disaster. The return across the meadow was a nightmare. I do not feel well enough to pursue the matter at present. I am tormented by a desire to know what the old crone did with it. That Fletcher woman has a lot to answer for. I'll make s . . . nobody else g . . .

'The end bit isn't very clear,' said Jamie. 'What do you make of it?'

Tom and Rosa said nothing.

'Don't you see? It's got to be about this place. What other cottage would you get to across the Florey's meadow?'

'Who's to say it's Florey's meadow?' said Tom.

'What other meadow would old Charles Florey write about?' said Jamie. 'It's *his* writing, and I can prove it. When I was clearing up after the break-in I found two letters of complaint he'd written to the shop. I don't know why Mum hung on to them. They were really nasty. He was disabled for years, you know, and *very* odd with it. This one must have been written just before he died.' He produced the crumpled letter from his other pocket. 'The date is February. Have a look. The writing is a perfect match.'

'It matches all right,' said Rosa, 'but ours isn't the only cottage that can be reached over the meadow. There's Black Nest next door and if you cut through Bluebell Wood you could get to the terrace on Main Street.'

'But you wouldn't find a Fletcher in them,' said Jamie.

It was clearly time to put Jamie in the picture. So they told him about Rosa's dreams, the dog incident and Ivy Wothers.

'I'm sorry,' he said, 'but I don't go in for all that fortune-telling and spooky stuff myself.'

'I know it sounds weird,' said Tom seriously, 'but we're not having you on.'

Jamie looked from Rosa to Tom and shrugged. They looked so earnest. 'I suppose there *might* be something in this Gift business,' he said, 'but I'm not convinced the dreams are connected.'

Then they showed him the paper they had found in the ashes. 'Same stuff,' he said. 'It's old Florey's diary. And it sounds as if your bit about getting something from "the old crone" comes first.'

'But he failed according to your bit,' said Rosa. 'It says, "the assault on the cottage was a disaster".'

'Hetty wouldn't have kept quiet about something like this,' said Tom.

'She did warn us off the Floreys,' said Rosa. 'And Giles Florey called me "one of you lot".'

'Charles Florey must have found out about The Gift,' said Tom. 'And Giles Florey has read it up in his diary.'

'Then why burn it in a place where we might find it?' said Rosa.

'Perhaps he doesn't know *you're* on to it,' said Jamie.

'He might have wanted to hide it from the staff. He sacked my Aunt Molly, didn't he?'

'He did have us watched for a bit,' said Rosa.

'Yes, but he won't have seen you looking for anything. You hadn't even heard of The Gift then.'

'We've got to hope he didn't see any of us looking in the ashes, then,' said Rosa.

But Tom had not forgotten the flash of light from the Manor window.

SIXTEEN

It was Jamie's idea to return to Wescombe.

'Tell Ivy Wothers that if she wants you to find this Gift she's going to have to say what it is. She might even believe it's you this time.'

They went straight to the alcove by the crazy golf where Rosa had spoken to Ivy. A tramp was in there, slouched against the wall with his eyes shut. He held a bottle of cider in his filthy hands and his chin was sore under the stubble.

'Excuse me,' said Jamie. 'Can you tell us if a fortune-teller has been here this morning?'

'Why on earth are you asking him?' said Tom. 'He might be dangerous.'

'What else have we got to go on?' said Rosa.

The man opened a bloodshot eye.

'Has Ivy Wothers been here?' said Rosa.

He opened the other eye and coughed revoltingly.

'We ought to go,' said Tom, 'and besides, I'm sure *he* won't know anything.'

'Can't think too easily,' the man said, looking furtively down the road for stray policemen. 'Not a drop of food 'as passed me lips today.'

His voice was slurred by alcohol and toothlessness. He sniffed, and wiped his nose on his dirty cuff.

'Here, have these,' said Jamie, producing a bag of salt and vinegar crisps.

The tramp took the bag grudgingly. 'S'pose it's better than nothing,' he said, pushing the bag into his frayed pocket.

Rosa was in no mood for games.

'We'd give you the price of breakfast if we didn't think you'd be straight down to the off-licence,' she said.

'Stop mucking about,' said Tom, 'and tell us if you've seen her. She's a little old lady called Ivy Wothers.'

The tramp seemed to be about to go into his wife-and-children-to-feed routine but obviously thought better of it.

'I 'aven't see nobody of that description 'ereabouts, miss. You might try the pier if you wants your fortune told. Waste of money them lot are though, if you ask me. I went to see that Neptune the Magnificent when I was a boy and he 'ad the nerve to tell me I would make no good of me life. Bloomin' idiot.'

It was a warm day and, although plenty of adults were sunning themselves along the pier, most small children were busy paddling in the muddy pools down on the beach, leaving the covered amusement arcade quiet.

Rosa led Tom and Jamie to the crane game.

'This is where I found the note,' she said. 'I suppose she *might* be near here, but I got the impression that she worked along the front.'

They scanned the hall but there was no sign of a fortune-teller.

'Lost someone?' said a man.

'We're looking for a fortune-teller,' said Tom.

'Sorry, mate,' said the man. 'There isn't one here, not that they'd 'ave many visitors today. Don't s'pose you saw any customers for me on your travels, did you?' He indicated his children's roundabout which stood idle.

'Sorry,' said Tom. 'The kids are all knee deep in mud and ice-cream out there. We'd need a crane to get any up for you.'

'We've heard there's a very good fortune-teller in Wescombe called Ivy Wothers,' said Rosa. 'Do you know where she works?'

'Can't 'elp you, love, but it might be worth asking Moses on bingo. He's worked 'ere for years and knows everybody. You can't miss 'im; small chap, white 'air.'

Moses was hanging a 'BACK SOON' sign on his stall.

'Want a go?' he said. 'I was just going for my tea break but I don't mind postponing it.'

'Not really,' said Rosa. 'We were hoping you could help us find someone.'

'Try me,' he said.

'Her name is Ivy Wothers and she tells fortunes.'

'Knew her for years,' he said. 'She used to work here. Some people swore by her; said she had a real gift. I doubt she matched her grandfather, though. He called himself Neptune the Magnificent. A real phenomenon he was – could have been the eighth Wonder of the World.'

'Where can we find Ivy?' said Tom.

'If I could tell you that, son, I'd be a rich man. She died some eleven years back, did Ivy.'

Rosa felt her knees sag. 'Died?' she said. 'She *can't* have.'

'Sorry, love, but that's the way it is. You'll not meet her now. I'll never forget how she kept working right until the end, even when she felt bad. She was so dedicated, I'm not surprised folks still talk about her. She gave me some good advice in her time.'

They thanked him. Rosa tried to keep calm. There must be a simple explanation for all this.

'Was the other lad your friend then?'

'Which lad?'

'A dark-haired youth — surly-looking chap. He was here asking questions about a week ago. Do you know him?'

'Yes,' said Tom grimly. 'I think we do.'

'Jake Florey,' said Jamie.

'Wasn't as polite as you three if you don't mind me saying so.'

'He wouldn't be,' said Tom. 'Sorry about that.'

'I don't suppose you can remember the exact day he was here, can you?' said Jamie.

Moses rubbed his chin thoughtfully. He didn't like to see the girl looking so upset.

'Must have been Thursday of last week. I had lots of customers and your young friend interrupted me. I know it was Thursday 'cause Bessie and Dolly Higgins were here. It's cut price for pensioners on Thursdays. Dolly was so shocked by your friend's manner she prodded him with her walking-stick and told him to be more polite to his elders. That any help?'

'It is a help, thank you,' said Rosa. 'But not at all what we expected.'

*

They took off their trainers and walked along the beach, past sunbathers on crumpled towels and ranks of brown sandcastles eroded by the warm wind.

'So Jake Florey was there before us,' said Tom. 'And on the day before the bonfire. What does it mean?'

'It means there *is* no Gift,' said Jamie gloomily. 'It's all been a blooming hoax; that creep Jake Florey has set us up. And there was me thinking he was too thick to set up so much as a game of snap.'

'Too right,' said Tom. 'Fancy having the patience to pretend to watch the cottage. He's obviously got nothing better to do with his summer holidays. He knew that spying game would get us interested. He tried burning a fake diary, and in case that didn't get to us he set up some old aunty of his to feed us a few false clues when we came to Wescombe.'

'He must have done his homework,' said Jamie. 'How ever did he know we were coming here? It was brilliant the way he got the note to Rosa.'

'What about the way he gave the old woman the names of Connie and Violet?' said Tom. 'You've got to admire his nerve, eh, Rosa?'

'And he even paid old Moses to lie to us in case we came snooping again. He must have got him to complain about his manners to make it sound genuine.'

Rosa stared incredulously at the boys.

'Stop it!' she shouted. 'Do you hear me?'

'Don't get upset,' said Tom. 'We've got plenty of time to plan our revenge. He needn't think he's going to get away with this little trick.'

'There *was* no trick, you idiots,' said Rosa. 'It's just too complicated. Do you really believe that moron would go to the trouble of making a perfect copy of his grand-father's writing? No way.'

The boys looked sympathetic but sceptical.

'I'm sure Moses was telling the truth,' she said. 'There must have been an Ivy Wothers.'

Her lower lip trembled.

'Rosa,' said Tom. 'If Moses *was* telling the truth about Ivy Wothers you must have been talking to a ghost. You don't believe *that*, do you?'

Rosa's face was ashen.

'Oh yes, she does,' said Jamie. A grin spread slowly over his face. 'This is getting really weird!'

SEVENTEEN

They took an early coach back from Wescombe. Tom wanted to tackle Moses before they left, but the others dissuaded him, Rosa because she was convinced that Moses *had* been telling the truth and Jamie because he still had a sneaking feeling it was a trick and didn't want Jake to know they'd found him out. However, they all agreed it would be better not to discuss The Gift until they were in a private place and decided they would return to Tanglewild together when they reached the village.

But Jamie's mother called him in as she saw him get off the village bus.

'I need your help,' she said. 'Sharee's gone off to the

dentist with raging toothache and I've got all the papers to get ready.'

So Tom and Rosa walked back to Tanglewild alone. It was Tom who spoke first.

'I wish I *could* believe you, Rosa, but this ghost business seems so impossible.'

'No more impossible than the idea of Jake using his brain,' she said.

'I know you've always had a way with animals,' he said, 'but talking to ghosts is another matter. If only we had some more evidence.'

As they walked past Dora Bishop's cottage they heard a mewing noise from above. Looking up, they saw Broom walking awkwardly along the roof, between closed dormer windows, with her left paws in the gutter and her right ones on the stone tiles.

'Silly puss,' called Rosa. 'How did you get up there?'

'She'll have a way down,' laughed Tom. 'Cats always do.'

'I'm not so sure,' said Rosa. 'She must have sneaked into the house and got out through the window. Dora will have shut her out when she took her bolster in.'

A loose tile creaked and Broom squatted low to keep her balance.

'She'll fall,' said Rosa, pushing open Dora's gate. 'I'm going to get her.'

'You're not going in *there*, are you?' said Tom.

'Why not?' she said. 'I've met a ghost this week, haven't I? Why be scared of Dora?'

She knocked on the door. Bonzo barked from within and a filthy net curtain was pulled back to reveal Dora's aggressive face. Her lower jaw stuck out like a shelf. Bonzo pressed his dirty face against the glass and made a wet mark with his silly nose.

'Go away,' shouted Dora. 'I don't know nothing.'

'Our cat's stuck on your roof. Please let me in so I can fetch her,' said Rosa.

'There's nothing on the roof. Nobody goes up there any more,' she shouted.

The curtain fell abruptly.

Rosa knocked again and Bonzo started throwing himself rhythmically against the front door. Broom yowled piteously from the roof.

'Please open the door, Miss Bishop.'

'Shan't,' shouted Dora.

Her childish voice gave Tom an idea. He strode up to the door and pushed open the letter flap, praying as he did so that Bonzo's nose would be too large to let him bite his fingers through the gap.

'Hello, Dora,' he said gently. 'We thought it was time we came to see you.'

No answer.

He could feel hot breath on his fingers as Bonzo sniffed enthusiastically around the open flap.

'We went to Wescombe today and saw the donkeys. I brought you some sweets. They're liquorice comfits. Do you like them?'

He produced a bag of comfits that Jamie had given him on the coach and rattled the packet. He and Rosa rarely touched sweets but in the strained atmosphere of the afternoon he hadn't had the heart to refuse them. Dora's eyes peered suspiciously through the open flap.

'I'd post them through,' he said, 'only Bonzo might get them.'

Bolts were pulled back, the door flung open and an eager hand reached out for the sweets.

Rosa pushed her way into the house but Dora barely noticed her. Instead she snatched the comfits and held them jealously to her bosom. 'Connie bought me sweeties in Wescombe,' she said, rocking from side to side as if she were cradling a baby.

Bonzo burst into the front garden to investigate the cat noises. He yelped ecstatically when he saw it was Broom but as he couldn't work out how to get up there with her he chased his dirty tail round and round in circles, until he lost his balance and fell in a patch of clover with his paws in the air.

Rosa stopped at the top of the stairs.

'Please come, Tom,' she said.

Her voice was strange.

'You go and enjoy your comfits while I help Rosa,' said Tom, gently pushing poor Dora into her living-room. 'You don't want the cat to bring down the gutters, do you? We'll get her for you.'

He joined Rosa at the top of the stairs. She was staring along the landing and Tom felt a heaviness in the air as he had on their first night at Hetty's. The layout of the cottage was identical to Tanglewild.

> Two doors were opposite each other near the end of the corridor. Both were closed. Beyond them, fixed to a beam, stood a wooden loft ladder. Above it was a trap door, also closed.

It was the ladder from Rosa's dream.

'We were meant to find it, Tom,' said Rosa.

'And we *must* go up there,' said Tom. 'Broom has given us the perfect excuse.' He called down the stairs to Dora: 'We'll see if we can get the cat in through the front window, Miss Bishop. If that fails we'll try the skylight in the loft, OK?' He hoped it wouldn't occur to her that the skylight was on the opposite side of the roof.

They pushed Dora's bedroom window open. The upper half of it was set above the gutter so Broom could easily have jumped up from the sill. Rosa sat on the sill and leaned out as far as she could.

'I can't see her,' she said. 'She must have fallen!'

'Let me look,' said Tom. 'The animal's not *that* stupid.'

Being taller, Tom managed to lean out a little further. Broom was up on the ridge tiles. She stood there like an Egyptian statue, with her whiskers flattened against her face by the wind.

'Come down, you silly creature,' he called. 'Not that way! She's gone over the top, Rosa. She's bound to walk past the skylight. We'll have to get her in that way after all. Quick!'

But by the time they had made their way across the loft and opened the skylight Broom was in the garden. It was Rosa who noticed her picking her way through the tall weeds along Dora's garden path.

'However did the silly animal get down there?' said Tom.

Rosa smiled.

'I should have known better than to underestimate a cat,' she said.

Tom walked back to the trap door. 'Here's a light switch,' he said. He pressed it.

It was only as she turned back into the loft that Rosa felt fear. It pressed in on her from all sides and seemed to crush the breath from her lungs.

An electric light bulb dangled down from the ridge. Spotlighted beneath it was a wooden table on which stood an old typewriter surrounded with piles of dusty books. Around the table was darkness, smooth oppressive darkness.

But Tom wasn't frightened.

'There's the typewriter,' he said. 'Just like you dreamed. It's filthy with dust.'

'Something happened up here,' said Rosa. 'Something bad. It looked like Hetty in my dream. It was night and very dark, but she had to put the light out. She was scared.'

'I don't think there's anything to be scared of now,' said Tom. He picked a book off the table and blew the dust off it. 'It's a dictionary,' he said, 'and the others are reference books. Not very interesting.'

Rosa felt calmer. 'There must be a clue here,' she said. 'What about those boxes?'

Apart from the table, a chair and the water tank they were the only things in the loft. There were four of them standing in a line beside the table, each named with a sticky label. Three seemed quite ordinary, being labelled:

POTS/PANS/SPARE CHINA
CLOTHES/SHOES
MAGAZINES/STAMP ALBUM, ETC.

But the third was worth investigating. It said:

VIOLET, 1958

The lid opened easily. Inside were personal items including a matching brush and mirror with polished wooden handles, a framed wedding photograph and a delicately crocheted shawl wrapped in thin paper. There was also a leather jewellery box in which they discovered a few pieces of paper: a theatre ticket for the Sladbury Playhouse, a recipe for home-made lemonade and a bundle of papers. These were letters of sympathy and small cards from Violet's funeral wreaths. On top was a card decorated all around with violets.

In memory of my darling Violet.
Time to leave your Black Nest.

'Let's go down,' said Rosa. 'We're prying.'

Tom lifted a pile of magazines from the box. Beneath them was a small painting in oils. It was exquisite.

'It's beautiful,' said Rosa. 'Look at the detail.'

It showed a pretty china bowl on a windowsill. In it were many delicate shells and tangles of dried seaweed and a lovely amber stone with a line of blue crystals set in it. Through the window was a view of rippling grey sea, so perfectly painted that Rosa could almost hear the waves. And out to sea a cloud of birds flew over a low black island. On the back of the frame were the words:

A Gift from the Sea, by Florence Miller
My dear Violet, remember me with this, Mother.

'It's by Florence Miller,' said Tom, peering at the front again. 'Never heard of her.'

'I wonder why not,' said Rosa. 'It's brilliant.'

'There's nothing else in here,' said Tom, pulling out some newspaper, 'just old books.'

There were a dozen books in all, arranged neatly across the bottom of the box.

'Virginia Booth,' said Rosa, leafing through one of them. 'Mummy's got them all. It's a pseudonym. Mummy says she was some sort of recluse who gave most of her profits to charity. Violet must have been keen on them too.'

She turned to the fly leaf. On it was the following dedication, written in ink:

Darling Albert, thank you for never
begrudging me the time to write,
your own Violet.

'Of course she liked them!' said Rosa. '*She* wrote them. The initials are the same.'

'It could be a coincidence,' said Tom. He looked in the other books. Each had a similar loving inscription. One said:

> *Thank you for sharing my little secret.*

'I *know* she wrote them,' said Rosa, 'and it was The Gift that made her so good. That must be why she gave away the profits.'

'Look at this one,' said Tom,

> *Here is my last novel, dearest.*
> *It is time to pass The Gift to another.*
> *Give Connie my letter at the time agreed.*
> *She will know what to do.*
> *Keep my secret, darling, and understand that*
> *I've told you so little to protect the little one,*
> *your loving Violet.*

A childish voice called up from through the trap door: 'I've saved you the red ones, Connie.'

'The "little one",' said Rosa, 'has got to be Dora.'

EIGHTEEN

When they returned to Tanglewild Hetty was not at home. Tom found the back-door key under an upturned bucket by the rockery and they let themselves into the kitchen. A note on the table said:

Lotty has had a fall and hurt her wrist.
Rod Johnson will drop us at casualty.
Make yourselves some sandwiches,
apple and elderberry tart on dresser.
I'll see Lotty to bed tonight so don't wait up.

yours, Hetty.

'Now what do we do?' said Tom.
'Just when we need to talk to her,' said Rosa.

'Will I do instead?' said Jamie, popping his head round the back door. 'I bet I will when you hear what I've got to tell you.'

'Go on, surprise us,' said Tom gloomily.

'There are three things,' he said. 'Which do you want first, the boring, the interesting or the very interesting?'

'Get on with it,' said Rosa.

Jamie looked hurt, but only for a moment.

'Firstly, and this is boring, Mum says please thank your Aunt Hetty for the fish tank. She's bought Boadicea a new arch to go with it and says Boadicea's a new fish.'

Rosa and Tom raised their eyes.

'Second, and this is interesting, the police are going to charge two Sladbury youths with our break-in. Apparently they caught them doing a video place over in the Sladbury arcade and they asked our job to be taken into consideration.'

'That rules out Jake Florey and his dad then,' said Tom.

'And third, and this is *really* interesting, something funny's going on at the Manor. I've just been chatting to Toby Dean. He left school last term and he does dispatch riding. He's just taken a parcel to the Manor and says Giles Florey looked as though he hadn't slept for days. He signed for the parcel all right but just chucked it on the hall stand, got in the Range Rover, cursing and swearing, and drove off down the drive at a hundred miles an hour.'

'Sounds like his normal behaviour to me,' said Tom.

'There's more,' said Jamie. 'Florey left his front door wide open and there was an odd hammering noise from upstairs.'

'Must have been Jake having a tantrum,' said Rosa.

'Toby said he stepped into the hall for a minute – he's a bit nosy like that – and thought he could hear someone shouting, "Let me out". He'd have gone further in, he said, only he could hear dogs barking. He says you can't be too careful with dogs.'

'Quite right,' said Tom.

'So what are we waiting for?' said Rosa. 'Florey is out of the way for a bit and we're not scared of Jake, are we? Let's get over there and find out what they're up to.'

'Are you barmy?' said Jamie.

'She's having one of her turns,' said Tom.

But they followed her just the same.

They set off to collect the bikes and on the way Rosa told Jamie what *they* had discovered.

'We're pretty sure Jake didn't hoax us,' said Rosa. 'We've been in Dora Bishop's house and seen her loft. It's the one I dreamed about, with the typewriter and everything. We know that Violet had The Gift and that she used it to help her write brilliant novels. We think she wanted her husband to give Connie a letter about it when the time was right. It must have told her to see Ivy Wothers. There was a note in her last novel about protecting the "little one". She didn't want Dora to know about The Gift and there must have been a good reason.'

'So who did Ivy give The Gift to?' said Jamie. 'And how on earth did Florey get to hear about it?'

'Do you think it *was* Dora?' said Tom. 'She could be the old crone Florey wrote about and the assault could have been on Black Nest. It ties in with Rosa's loft dreams.'

'But Florey mentioned a Fletcher,' said Jamie, 'and your aunt was in one dream. What if *she* had The Gift?'

'Even if we knew it was either of those,' said Rosa, 'it wouldn't tell us who's got The Gift now. Ivy said it was in safe hands, but we must find it before anybody else.'

'But what the heck are we looking for?' said Jamie.

'That's what we all want to know,' said Tom.

'Perhaps we'll find the answer at the Manor,' said Rosa grimly.

The Manor door was open as Toby Dean had described. Dirty boots, unopened letters and newspapers littered the hall floor and muffled barking came from within. Rosa walked into the house.

'It's all right, girls,' she called. 'It's only me.'

The barking, which came from a door to the left, subsided to a whimper. The boys followed Rosa into the hall.

'There's something wrong,' said Rosa. 'I'm going to open the door.'

'She knows what she's doing,' said Tom, hoping she did.

Behind the door was the kitchen. Once a grand room and expensively furnished, it was now a picture of neglect. Filthy crockery and empty bottles lay in precarious piles on the table and broken china crunched underfoot.

The barking came from behind another door. As Rosa opened it the dogs burst out, licking her face, nuzzling her and pushing their thin bodies as close to her as they could. They had been in a tiny walk-in broom cupboard and, judging by the stench and desperate scratch marks on the door, they had been shut in there for days.

'They're starving,' she said. 'Find some food.'

Jamie found a box of Doggo Crunch.

'That'll do for a start,' she said. 'I'll get some water.'

There was mould on the dog bowls so they used baking tins from one of the cupboards.

When the dogs had eaten they nudged Rosa's legs and looked up at her with urgent brown eyes.

'What is it, girls?' she said.

The animals padded to the door and waited.

'They want you to follow them,' said Tom. 'Come on.'

So the three children followed the dogs across the hall, up the stairs and along the landing until they stopped outside a closed door. Tom tried the handle.

'Locked,' he said.

He hammered on the door. The dogs whimpered.

'Who's in there,' shouted Jamie. 'Open up.'

'Get me out of here,' came the reply. It was Jake.

'Hurry up, you morons,' he said. 'He could be back any minute. The spare key's on a hook in the kitchen; it's the one with the green plastic tab.'

Rosie nodded to Jamie to go and fetch the key.

'This had better not be a trick, Florey,' said Tom.

There was no reply and he wished his knees didn't feel so wobbly.

When they entered Jake was standing with his back to them, gazing out of his window towards Black Nest. Jamie shut and locked the door behind them.

'You don't get out of here until we have a few answers, Florey,' he said. He felt a dramatic gesture like swallowing the key was called for but made do with putting it in his pocket.

'Can't you face us, Florey?' said Tom.

Rosa said nothing but patted the dogs' heads reassuringly. There was sadness in the room.

'We want to know why you have been spying on us, Florey, why your grandad bullied Dora Bishop and why you and your father have been burning things in the meadow,' said Tom.

'And *I* want to know why my aunt got the sack,' said Jamie.

'Why are you up here?' said Rosa.

'It's a trick, isn't it?' said Jamie. 'You don't fool us.'

Jake's shoulders began to shake.

'He's laughing,' said Jamie. 'I *knew* it. It's a trick. Turn round, you creep.'

Jake turned. His face was wet with tears.

'He's blubbing!' said Jamie. 'Are you scared, Florey? A great bully like you?'

Tom felt embarrassed. 'Tell us about The Gift, Florey,' he said. 'We know you're on to it.'

Rosa felt dizzy.

'. . . help from an unexpected source.'

'You *wanted* us to come, didn't you?' she said. 'Who locked you in here?'

'My father,' said Jake. 'I wanted you to find me, but I could hardly bring myself to shout for help after the way I treated you last week.'

'You'd better sit down,' said Tom awkwardly.

Jake sat on the edge of his rumpled bed.

'I know a bit about The Gift,' he said gruffly, 'but I don't *want* it. It's my father you want to worry about. I wish you'd got here sooner. He's determined to find it. He's got to be stopped.' He stood again and looked anxiously out of the window. 'He might be back any minute. Get me out of here and I'll tell you all I know.'

'What are we waiting for?' said Tom. 'Let's get out of here.'

'He'd better be telling the truth,' said Jamie.

'We haven't got time to worry about that,' said Tom. 'Where shall we take him?'

'Back to Tanglewild, of course,' said Rosa. 'I hope you've got a bike, Jake.'

When they had left Jake's room Jamie locked the door and returned the key to its hook.

'We've got to make it look as if nobody's been here,'

said Tom. 'Jamie and Jake could be getting the bikes sorted while we deal with the dogs.'

'I'm not shutting them in that prison again,' said Rosa.

'Let's clear up the baking tins and leave the door open as if they've escaped then,' said Tom. 'But hurry up!'

'The poor things will have to follow us all the way to Hetty's,' said Rosa, 'but at least we'll be able to find them some decent food there.'

'If we get there,' said Tom. 'It would be just our luck to bump into Giles Florey.'

NINETEEN

When they reached Tanglewild Jake and Jamie sat in chintz armchairs in the sitting-room while Rosa fed the dogs. Jamie had borrowed some dog food from the shop and told his mother not to expect him until later. Tom poured glasses of home-made grape crush and cut wedges of apple and elderberry tart which they ate with chunks of Double Gloucester cheese. Outside a blackbird sang from the top of the apple tree and in the sitting-room Broom and the dogs curled up together on the rug. To an outsider it would have looked quite ordinary, but the story Jake was about to tell was far from ordinary. He didn't mention The Gift straight away and they didn't rush him.

'My grandad is to blame for getting me into all this,' said Jake. 'He made our lives a misery when he was alive and is still doing it now he's dead.'

'It can't have been easy being disabled for so long,' said Rosa.

'His accident had a lot to do with it. I was only three but I'll never forget it. He had a fall one night. My father could never get him to say what had happened, but *someone* knew. They left him outside the front door on a ladder they'd used as a stretcher. It looked as if he'd got away with cuts and bruises at first, but we sent him to hospital anyway. He was taken bad there with a brain haemorrhage. It turned out he'd bumped his head when he fell. They kept him in for weeks. His left arm and leg weren't much good after that. When he came home he was in a really bad way and very bitter about his accident. My mother had furnished a room for him downstairs and she and my father tried to make him comfortable, but he'd have nothing to do with us unless it was to cause trouble. He spent most of his time writing away in his diaries. He hated us all.'

'Did he blame you in some way?' asked Rosa.

'That's just what I asked my mother. She said he'd *always* been a bitter man. Something to do with a bad experience he'd had when he was a boy.'

'It must have been *some* experience,' said Jamie, who had heard all sorts of rumours about Charles Florey.

'His father died really poor,' said Jake. 'You wouldn't think so to look at our house, would you? He'd been chucked out of his job at Forest Mill and was so skint Grandad's mother couldn't give him a decent funeral. Grandad felt really ashamed about it, and when he saw the rich mill-owners with their posh houses and fancy clothes it made him bitter and very odd. He was determined that he was going to make money. He saw it as a way of getting his own back on the world.'

'I thought Floreys had always been in the Manor,' said Tom.

'No way. It was Grandad who bought it. He clawed his way up, got into business and managed to make pots of money. He even married rich. They were living in London when Dad was born, but Grandad wasn't happy there. Being rich wasn't enough. He wanted power. When Nettlebury Manor came up for sale he bought the place and played at being the lord of the manor.'

'Mum said there was a lot of fuss about him buying up the cottages in the village,' said Jamie.

'That's right. He was really ruthless, bought out the owners of those terraced cottages and then charged huge rents. Everybody hated him.'

'What did your grandma make of it?'

'She left him in the end.'

'Had your dad got married then?' asked Jamie.

'Yes, and when Grandma left Grandad started to take it out on my mother. He hated her, said she was beneath my dad and tried to cause trouble between them whenever he could. What made matters worse was that his business ventures started to go wrong. It got so bad that he was forced to sell the cottages. My guess is that he'd been cheating people and they'd got wise to him. When my parents decided to leave the Manor Grandad made all sorts of threats about cutting them out of his will. My father was really worried about that but my mother said she'd rather be poor and happy. Of course they didn't feel they *could* leave after Grandad's accident.'

'Your mum must have told you all this,' said Tom. 'What happened to her?'

'She died,' said Jake. 'I was ten.'

'You must miss her,' said Rosa gently.

'So does Dad. I think that's what's made him the way he is. He pretends he doesn't care and says awful things about her, but I know he misses her. He seemed to crumble when she went. He rents out the land and deals with the stables, but he can't cope without her and gets in a temper when things go wrong – especially when he drinks a lot. I'm just scared he's going to go mad like my grandad.'

'What was your grandad like at the end?' asked Rosa.

'He got senile. He'd kept up a bit of business, something to do with wine importing, and was dealing with some very shady looking characters, but got so vague in the end that they stopped coming.'

'What was he like to you?' asked Jamie.

'He didn't seem to know we were there. It was a relief in a way. At least he stopped complaining. He just sat in his chair and rambled on to himself. That's when my father first got wind of this Gift business. Grandad would say things like: "They're well hidden. I've seen to that. I'm damned if anybody else is going to get their hands on it." I took no notice, but my father was convinced he'd made big money with his shady wine business and had it stashed away somewhere in the Manor.'

'That's why he started to search the place after your grandad died,' said Jamie. 'But why did he sack my aunty?'

'He got worried that someone else was going to find the treasure before he did. He even treated *me* worse, if that's possible. It's been best to keep out of his way as much as possible these last few months. I have tried to keep an eye on the horses but I got fed up with clearing up *his* mess. Let him rot, I thought.

'I did make an exception, though, just before Tom and Rosa arrived here, when he'd chucked a pile of books through a window in Grandad's room. The rain was coming in so I decided I'd better get Rod Johnson in to repair it. If I hadn't asked him I'd never have heard of The Gift.'

The atmosphere in the room changed to one of tense anticipation. Broom sensed it and sat erect with her ears pricked up.

'Please tell us about it, Jake,' said Rosa. 'We need to know as much as possible.'

'When Rod had finished the window he asked me if I'd like him to look at a sagging floorboard in the corner. He said there might be a bit of wet rot there so we pulled up the carpet. But it wasn't rot. There was a loose board and underneath it we found a cardboard box. I had a look inside and saw it was Grandad's diaries. Goodness knows who he got to put them in there, but he obviously didn't want us to get hold of them. I knew my father would be livid. He was hoping for hidden treasure and all he had was a box full of junk. I thought he'd throw it away so I took one diary for myself. I don't know why I wanted it; Grandad cared as little about me as my father.

'My father was furious when he saw the box and I wished I'd chucked it away. He accused me of being in league with my grandad and pulled up all the loose floorboards in the room to find the loot I'd hidden. Next he decided the money was in the journals. He took them up to his room and said I was to keep out or else. I think he was expecting to find bank notes between the pages.

'He obviously found *something* in the books, but it wasn't money. He got out his binoculars and started peering out of the house towards the village. When he realized he couldn't see much at that distance he sent me to the meadow with instructions to write down everything that happened at the two cottages on Gozzards Reach. When I asked what he was after he said I couldn't be trusted with that information. He also made a few of his nasty remarks about my mother. That always gets to me; I expect that's why I was so rough with Tom when you came trespassing on our land.

'When I told my father you'd seen me he was livid. He shouted a lot and hit me. That was when I decided I was through with him. It was time to find out what he was up to. And if he was on to something that was worth having I'd get it for myself.

'I went into his room that night. He was out drinking again so I had plenty of time. There were diaries dating back to the year after Grandad's accident so I took that one first. My father had been through the entries circling any that interested him. They were mostly references to business matters and that sort of thing, but one mentioned the fall. Grandad had written how bitter he was about the accident at the cottage and that if the crone had been alone he'd be rich by now. He said he should have had his men watching Gozzards Reach long before he went in. He'd been too impatient and that had lost him everything.

'So, you see, my father was watching the cottages thirteen years after Grandad's accident in the vain hope of discovering hidden treasure. What a fool.

'It was only when I looked through the diary I had taken that I began to realize what Grandad had been up to. My mother had hired Dora Bishop a few months before Grandad's accident. She was known in the village as being a bit simple but my mother had noticed an improvement in her and was prepared to give her a chance at the cleaner's job. Grandad was determined to prove my mother wrong, as he was with anything she did, and decided to get Dora drunk. One day he offered her some wine left over from his lunch. She got a bit giggly on it and said blackcurrant juice had never done that to her before, but he was surprised to find her quite coherent, almost witty. When he asked her why she seemed so different that night she said it was because she was using her little secret. My grandad was keen on secrets, especially if they sounded as though they might do *him* some good, so he gave her more wine.

'She told him she had been given a little gift that helped her to get her thoughts straight and that anybody else who had it would be able to do something better too. At first he thought she was on about some sort of medicine her doctor had given her, but as she spoke it began to sound far more interesting.

'She said that her father had died suddenly and although he had been seventy-five he had not got round to sorting out his affairs. Not that she wanted for anything; an allowance had been fixed for her by her mother a few years back. Among his personal things she had found a sealed envelope addressed to Connie Dornan. It was in her mother's handwriting and as she had been dead for years she thought it would do no harm to look at it. What she found made her very jealous. It said something about a precious gift that was waiting for Connie in Wescombe. Her mother wrote that she could not give it to Dora; Connie would understand why. She must see Ivy Wothers in Wescombe and all would be revealed. Dora told Grandad she had hidden the letter from Connie and had got more and more jealous as she tried to guess what present her mother had left for Connie. She decided she'd *never* tell Connie about it and if she ever had the chance she would get the present for herself.

'She didn't trust Connie so much after that but Connie was as kind as ever and took her out for an Easter treat to Wescombe. Dora soon found Ivy Wothers working on the pier. She was a fortune-teller, granddaughter of the mighty Neptune or something. When she got in there she showed Ivy the letter and said, "I've come for what's mine." Ivy thought she was talking to Connie and gave Dora The Gift, no questions. Seemed she couldn't wait to get rid of it. Dora wouldn't tell my grandad what it was but said it had changed her life.

'Grandad put the pressure on her. He was a greedy old man. He probably thought Dora's secret would help him to make more money and get the respect he felt he deserved from the villagers. But The Gift must have made Dora a bit cunning and she wouldn't tell him another thing. He wasn't one to give up that easily, though. He sent a couple of men in to frighten her. They bullied her a bit and tipped a few books and things on the floor. They were upstairs when your Aunt Hetty came in from next door. They told her they were checking for rats. She sent them packing, but not before they had time to notice how agitated Dora became when they went anywhere near the loft ladder.

'When they reported this to my grandad he was triumphant. He was convinced he had discovered the hiding place for The Gift. He was annoyed that Hetty had been involved. She could be a nuisance, and was so determined that neither she nor anyone else should get to know about Dora's secret that he decided to return that night. He had an insane plan to get into the loft by the skylight.

'He walked across the fields to the back of the cottage and was hoping he'd be able to sneak in and out without anybody knowing. It was a misty night and he was delighted to find Black Nest in darkness. Although he had the two men with him to carry the ladder he insisted upon climbing up on the roof. He wasn't going to let anybody else get their hands on The Gift. He got on the roof, crawled up to the skylight and shone his torch on it to work out where to stick the crowbar. That was when he got the shock of his life. Dora was there peering out at him and she had someone behind her; *"probably that Fletcher woman"*, he wrote. It startled him so much that he lost his footing and slid down the roof. He was badly hurt, but insisted that the men had to carry him over the fields on the ladder rather than be discovered in Dora's garden. He wouldn't even let them call an ambulance until he was home.

'It's no wonder the old fool was so bitter. When he got back from hospital he must have spent all his time wishing he'd got his hands on The Gift, but because he was so mean he couldn't bear to tell anybody else about it. That must be why he hid the diaries under the floor.

'Once I knew what it was all about I was surprised by what I felt. I thought I'd want the thing my father was after for myself. A bit of extra cash would have come in handy — I'll be old enough to start driving soon and I could use a decent car — but this Gift sounded a bit dicey to me. Dora had got herself bullied because of it and my grandad was disabled. I could just imagine what it would do to my father. I had to make sure he never got to know about it. I did wonder if the whole thing was a hoax; Grandad was a bit odd, but I didn't think he could have dreamed up something so weird.

'I started by going to Wescombe. If Ivy Wothers still worked there I wanted to have a word with her. It was the day you had a go at my father outside the shop. We went into Sladbury together, but instead of meeting him in the car park as planned I took the Wescombe coach. It gave me a real shock to find out the old woman had snuffed it, but at least she *had* existed. This meant that my grandad had not invented that bit of the story. From what the chap on the pier said, Ivy Wothers must have died soon after Dora saw her, and it was pretty amazing Dora met her at all as Ivy was at least eighty by then and only worked on her good days. When I got over the shock I felt quite relieved. If *I* couldn't see her, then neither could my father.

'I got home after twelve that night having spent as long as I could wandering about Sladbury. Father was asleep in a chair in Grandad's room and had obviously been drinking. I don't know what got into me when I saw him there. I think it was fear. I had this strong feeling that when he woke up he would be able to tell I knew something and he wouldn't rest until he found out what it was.

'I was pretty sure I could keep quiet about what I knew, even if he got rough, but I had to make sure he'd never see the diaries again, especially the one *I* took. I decided the only thing to do was to burn the lot, but I knew I mustn't do it at the Manor in case he woke up. I quickly got the box of diaries from his room, along with the one I'd taken, and put them in the back of the Range Rover. There was a bale of straw in there that would go up well and I bunged in a heap of newspapers from the hall for good measure.

'I'd started up the engine before I thought of petrol and matches. I was terrified he'd hear me and would stop me from leaving the house. He was pretty far gone though and I managed to get the stuff and race off down the drive. The Range Rover must have made quite a row. I couldn't cope with the gears. I'd had a go in it on our land a couple of times but I hadn't been in a hurry then.

'I went to the meadow. It meant opening a couple of gates, but I would be far enough away from the house to get a good blaze going without having to leave our land. I knew anybody from the cottages or Stinchampton Common would be able to see the fire if they happened to be looking out at that time in the morning. Perhaps I hoped there'd be a witness. The way my father had been acting recently I wouldn't have put it past him to do something nasty.

'I waited out on the meadow until everything had burned. It was a bit windy so it went up a treat. I found a bit of old angle iron in the Range Rover to use as a rake and made sure it had burned right down before I went back to the Manor.

'He was waiting for me when I went in. He knew I'd taken the diaries and he had seen the fire. He wasn't the least bit worried that I might have had an accident in the Range Rover. Perhaps he wished I had. He looked as though he was going to kill me anyway. Instead he threw me in my room and locked the door.

'That was a week ago. He came in every so often to try to bully information out of me but I acted dumb, as if I hadn't a clue what he was talking about. He gave me the odd bit of food if he remembered but after a day or two he lost interest in me. I have my own bathroom (although it pongs like the rest of the house) so there was no problem with drinks, but the only food I had was half a packet of chocolate digestives and a couple of apples and they didn't last for long. He went out a lot but when he was in I could hear him rampaging about the house searching for clues. He let the dogs out a couple of times, but after that I could hear them whining and scratching from the kitchen. The worst thing is that I think he sold the horses, including my horse Blade. I saw the animals being collected and there was nothing I could do about it. He must need the money. No wonder he's going frantic about this Gift business.

'I tried to get the milkman's attention, but he leaves the bottles at the yard gate since my father swore at him and I couldn't get him to hear me. The postman came three times, but always when my father was in, so that was no help. I thought I might be in luck when I saw you snooping about the ashes. I saw Jamie first. The next morning Tom and Rosa came. It was sunny so I tried to flash the light off my mirror to get your attention. It always works in books, doesn't it? But you didn't seem to notice. I wished I hadn't burned the stuff so well. I prayed you'd find a clue that would lead you there.

'If Toby Dean hadn't been so nosy I'd still be there now.'

'So now what do we do?' asked Jamie.

'We wait for Hetty,' said Rosa.

TWENTY

They were helping themselves to more food when Hetty got home. The tart was finished so Tom was cutting hunks of bread to go with the remains of the cheese, while Rosa spooned Hetty's home-made pickle on to the plates. It was very late, but if Hetty was surprised to see them up she didn't show it.

'Had an energetic day?' she said.

'Not half,' said Tom. 'Want some?'

'No thank you, dear, I had a light supper with Lotty. They've strapped up her wrist and she assures me she can manage by herself tonight. I told her I didn't like to think of you being in the cottage alone at night.'

She looked at the four plates.

'Got company, have we?'

'Yes,' said Rosa. 'And we need to talk to you.'

Hetty insisted that Jamie should ring his mother to let her know he was safe. She would have had Jake doing the same had the children not assured her that it would be very dangerous for him to do so. Half an hour later they had told her all they knew.

'What you have told me has shed some light on many things that have happened in the cottages,' she said. 'As far as Jake is concerned, I shall see to it that the cruelty will stop. There are people trained to help with such matters. I shall contact someone first thing in the morning. And as for the other matter, I think I shall tell you what *I* know. But first Rosa must make a decision as to who should hear it.'

'Don't worry, I'll go, Miss Fletcher,' said Jake. 'I don't expect to be trusted after the way I treated Tom and Rosa the other day, but I'm not going back to the Manor.'

'He could go in my room while we talk,' said Tom.

'Good idea,' said Jamie. 'But what about me?'

'Everybody stays,' said Rosa. 'We're all in this. Jake's father might have been asking questions in the village. Someone could easily have seen us and it wouldn't do to bump into him in the dark. It's got to be safer if we stick together tonight. Jamie had better ring his mother again and ask if he can stop for the night.'

Her tone was such that nobody disagreed and they soon settled down to listen to Hetty.

'I first saw Violet and Albert Bishop a few weeks before they were married. She was called Violet Miller then. They were young and blissfully happy. They loved the village and were delighted with the cottage. They thought it was the perfect home, pretty yet spacious enough for a family, and they planned to move in as soon as they were married. Violet was really taken with the countryness of Nettlesfield. She had been brought up in Little Wescombe. It's further along the estuary than Wescombe and quite bleak, from what I've heard. She spoke of the place with affection, but after they'd settled here I never heard of her going back once.

'When they moved in she named the cottage Black Nest; I never knew why. They didn't bring much furniture with them, but I remember that picture you found. It used to hang downstairs when Violet was alive. Connie was fascinated by it; she'd kneel up on a chair and peer into it, counting the shells and seeing how many different corals there were. Violet told her it was the view from a window of her home in Little Wescombe and that her mother had painted it for her. Connie asked lots of questions about it. She wanted to know if Florence Miller had done any other paintings and if she could see them. That was the only time I saw Violet be sharp with Connie. Perhaps she was still grieving for her mother; she'd not been dead long. I must have been five and Connie was nine when they came, and we liked Violet straight away. She had a look about her – an aura if you like, but it was Connie who really got to know her. Connie had a real gift with people even at that age and the Bishops welcomed her into their house as if she were their own.

'It was two years later that Dora was born. There were complications and they feared she would not survive, but she was a tough little thing and pulled through against all odds. Violet and Albert loved her dearly even though she was a bit simple, but it was Connie who knew just how to deal with her. She was very patient with her and it was a delight to see the way she brought her on.

'Violet was busy a lot of the time. She went upstairs for hours on end. I thought she was in the spare bedroom. They'd kept it nice for the second child they'd never had, but from what you've told me she must have been doing her writing in the loft. I'm sure it was brilliant, but in the summer I was mystified as to what she could want to do in her cottage when it was so lovely outside.

'Our mum must have been fifty when Dad died, and a few years after that Connie went off to marry Harold. They went to live in Hampton Leonard so they were never far away. Dora missed her terribly, but Connie was a kind soul and called in whenever she could, sometimes bringing a treat with her.

'By the time Connie was expecting Grace, Dora was nearly twenty. She was gawky and unattractive and had no hope of finding herself a husband. It's not important, *I* should know that, but it mattered to Dora. She was so desperate to be like Connie that Grace's birth caused a rift between them. Connie was as gentle as ever with Dora, but of course she was busy with the baby. You couldn't help but notice Dora's resentment.

'When Grace was about eleven Violet died. It was one March. I remember it vividly as all the nests blew out of the elm trees up Swallow Lane. It was another downhill step for Dora to lose her mother. Her face was always a little sadder after that. Albert did his best for her, I tried to keep an eye on her and Connie used to visit when she could. She brightened up a bit when Connie moved back to Tanglewild but they were never as close as they were before Connie married. Albert died in 1974, some sixteen or so years after Violet. That must be when Dora found the letter to Connie. I can understand her jealousy. Violet *had* loved Dora deeply but found it hard to relate to her. Her fondness for Connie was expressed with far more ease. It must have devastated Dora to read about a present that must go to Connie instead of her.

'I remember noticing the change in her. Connie persuaded her to go on a seaside trip, the Easter after Albert died, a sort of treat to cheer her up. It was after that that Dora seemed to pick up. She was more confident and seemed to be able to express herself more clearly. She even took on a charring job at the Manor, something she could never have coped with before. Though we were delighted to see Dora so happy, Connie felt uneasy. She didn't know why, but she sensed something was not as it should be.

'Things were so much better that I was surprised, when I called round one day, to find Dora in a dreadful state. A couple of Florey's men were intimidating her and messing up her belongings. When I challenged them they kept wittering on about vermin infestation. I told them that *they* were the only vermin I had seen in the vicinity and sent them packing.

'If I'd known what you've told me about Charles Florey and his plans I'd never have left Dora that day. As it happened she wasn't alone when he came. Connie had been out for the day and must have called in at Black Nest on her way home.

'She never got here. I'd gone to bed early otherwise I'd have been worried about her. The first thing I knew was when I found Dora hammering on my door in the middle of the night. She said to come to Black Nest quickly because Connie had been taken bad. I left Dora here with instructions to ring for an ambulance, and hoped she would manage it. She begged not to be left alone, but I was frightened for Connie and had to be firm. I found Connie in Black Nest at the bottom of the loft ladder. She had suffered some sort of attack. It was such a shock to see her so breathless and clammy. She was conscious, but only just. She said it had taken some time to persuade Dora to fetch me. I told her to save her breath, but she wanted to tell me something.

'She said Dora hadn't answered the door when she

called round. She sensed something was wrong and let herself in. She'd always had a key since Albert died. Dora was up in the loft and refused to come down. She begged Connie to stay with her that night – said someone was coming and that she had to hide. I can still remember her words. She said: "It was getting dark, but she made me put the light out, Hetty. He was coming . . . the creaking frightened me, Hetty, but I had to look after Dora. He's hurt . . . but there's someone with him . . . they'll help."

'She'd always been afraid of the dark. Never grew out of it. I think it must have been Connie that Rosa saw in her dream. We always did look alike.

'I asked her who had come but she started to shake and couldn't answer.

'"Dora's told me about it now . . . He didn't get it, Hetty, but she gave it to me too late. Take it . . ."

'It made little sense to me but I nodded to reassure her. I could hear Dora coming.

'"In my pocket," she said. Her voice was just a whisper now. "Get it before they take me, put it somewhere safe, then leave it well alone . . . Promise me, Hetty."

'So I emptied her pockets and she said no more . . . I could hear the ambulance sirens . . . and Dora came, screaming . . . I managed not to cry . . .

'It wasn't until the next year that I discovered what she was talking about. It was August and I'd been feeling very low since Connie's death. I decided to pull myself out of it and took a trip to Wescombe. I did everything, ice-cream, a deckchair on the front and a look round the amusements. That was when I saw Ivy Wother's tent. The name meant nothing to me, but I thought it might be amusing to go in. She was a dear old lady, just as Rosa has described. She took me by the hand and I could feel her trembling.

' "Is it you, Hetty?" she said. "Connie gave you something. I'll not mention its name as I've been tricked once. I hope you've got it safe. There'll be a newborn. Give it to her when she's ready. She'll come to you. And you must decide if the time is right. It helped you that night, but don't touch it again. It's meant for the newborn. Just keep it safe."

'I've always thought these people relied on trickery, but I was quite impressed that she knew our names. Connie *had* given me something, but you could say that about many people and be right. There had only been one thing in Connie's pocket that looked important and I knew that it was in a safe place. Although I understood little else of what she had said, I've never forgotten her words . . . never.'

'So you've had The Gift all along,' said Jamie.

'That is for Rosa to discover,' said Hetty.

'Aren't you going to tell us what it is?' said Tom. 'What do you say, Rosa? Are we all in on this too?'

'I don't know what to do,' said Rosa eventually. 'Ivy told me I was the only person who could save The Gift, but it has taken four of us to get this far. Ivy said I would have help from an unexpected source – that must be Jake – but that I shouldn't let anyone get there first.'

'You're very young,' said Hetty. 'It's been thrust upon you too soon, because of the things that went wrong. I knew you had unnatural gifts from when you were a toddler. The animals would come to you even then. They trusted you. I'll never forget that fox that took a walk through my garden. You went to it as if it were a harmless puppy and it licked your hand.'

'Yes,' said Tom, hoping to make Rosa smile. 'She's always been funny like that.'

But Rosa had not heard him. Instead she sat stiff and

erect, her face frozen and unnatural. The dogs whimpered and Broom's tail swished from side to side. Tom felt again the heavy feeling he had known on the night of Rosa's nightmare.

'Look at *her*,' said Jamie. 'She's in a trance.'

'I'm getting out of here,' said Jake.

'Sit down and be quiet,' said Hetty firmly.

So they waited to see what would happen.

> *'It only works by touch,'* said Rosa. *'But the power lingers.'*

Was it *her* voice?

> *'Don't let anyone get there first.'*

Jake coughed nervously and Tom dug him in the ribs with his elbow.

> *'Don't trust the wrong person or someone will be in danger.'*
> *'It's in safe hands but she doesn't understand the dangers.'*
> *'Only* **you** *can save The Gift.'*

And then Rosa was herself again.

'What do you make of that?' said Jamie.

'Call me soft if you like,' said Jake. 'But I don't like it.'

They looked at Rosa.

'I've got to go on alone, haven't I?' she said.

'Are you sure?' said Hetty.

Rosa nodded.

Hetty told the boys to clear up, took Rosa up to her room and closed the curtains. It was a tranquil place. The air was fragrant from pot-pourri and lavender bags, its floral wallpaper was comfortably faded and every shelf and table top was busy with memories – a photograph of

Great-granny Winifred, postcards from holidays, favourite books and little pots on lace mats.

Rosa sat on the edge of the bed. Its firmness was comforting.

'Let me tell you what I found in Connie's pockets, dear,' said Hetty, holding Rosa's smooth hand in her wrinkled one. 'When that is done you may do what you will with the information. You're young, but you'll know what's for the best.'

Rosa felt nervous, but strangely excited.

'In one of Connie's pockets was her lace hanky. I'd given it to her the Christmas before and embroidered "CONNIE" on it myself. I have it in my dressing-table drawer if you wish to see it. There was also a shopping list which I threw away. In the other pocket was a shiny stone. Connie liked pretty things. I couldn't bear to keep it. I threw it out of my back door that night they took my Connie away . . . and then I cried . . .'

'Was there anything else?' said Rosa.

'This,' said Hetty. She opened a little drawer in her bureau and pulled out a white envelope addressed to Connie Dornan. 'It's open, but I've never read it. I left it well alone, just as I promised Connie.'

She put the envelope on the bed next to Rosa.

'I'll not say any more about it now, dear,' she said. 'The rest must come from you.'

She turned to leave.

'Stay in my room tonight. I'll make sure you're not disturbed. But do think carefully before you make any decisions.'

When Hetty had left Rosa picked up the envelope and slid out the letter. It said:

> *My Dear Connie,*
> *I hope that, in his grief, Albert will remember to*
> *give this to you. He knows little about its contents. I*

am leaving you a precious gift. It waits for you with a dear friend, Ivy Wothers, in Wescombe. Tell her who you are and she will know what to do. It was a gift from the sea, given to my mother by Neptune the Magnificent. My mother left it with Ivy for me, but sadly I dare not give it to my little Dora. You will understand why, dear Connie. Use it well and keep it safe,

> *Yours, Violet.*

Rosa lay on Hetty's bed to think. A shopping list, a new hanky, a stone and a letter. Which was The Gift? The letter was not. But it *told* of a gift, given to Violet's mother. She remembered Florence Miller's beautiful painting: *A Gift from the Sea*. It showed a bowl containing delicate shells and corals, twists of weed and a lovely amber stone with a line of blue crystals set in it.

Rosa knew that if she could find that stone she would have found The Gift.

TWENTY-ONE

Jamie woke early to an enthusiastic dawn chorus. He was curled up stiffly on Hetty's sofa under a prickly wool rug. He stretched his legs over the end of the sofa, knocking Broom, who had been sleeping on his ankles, on to the floor. She gave him a superior look and sat instead beside the sleeping dogs on the rug.

'I don't know, Broom,' said Jamie, as he thought over the events of the last few days. 'Life seemed quite ordinary until the Howells came to Nettlesfield.'

Broom licked a paw.

'I don't really go for all that supernatural stuff myself,' he said, wiggling his feet in the hope of getting the feeling back. 'But Rosa is really weird. I just hope she'll know how to handle this Gift, if it's around. Everybody else seems to have made a bit of a mess of it.'

Later he decided to get breakfast. The dogs came bounding into the kitchen as soon as they heard cutlery chinking so he fed them first. Broom slept; she had spent most of the night hunting. There seemed to be a distinct shortage of food apart from half a wholemeal loaf (which was very dry at the edges) and a bowl of eggs.

'Easy,' he said. 'Boiled eggs and toast.'

Nobody spoke much over breakfast. Jake had neck ache from sleeping on the put-you-up, Hetty was discreetly scraping the toast outside the back door and the others were busy scooping the blobs of congealed egg white from the outside of the cracked eggs.

'Nice cup of tea,' said Tom when they had finished.

Jamie grinned sheepishly.

'I'm lost without a tin of spaghetti shapes,' he said.

Rosa ate nothing.

After breakfast she told them that she wanted to be alone at Tanglewild. It was decided that Jamie should take Tom, Jake and the dogs round to his flat. They would keep a look-out for Jake's father from there and Tom made Rosa promise she would ring for help if she needed it.

Hetty left soon afterwards.

'I shall leave you now,' she said briskly. 'I have to visit poor Lotty and see how her wrist is healing. There'll be shopping to do for her and I must stock up on a few essentials myself judging by the number of visitors I seem to be having at the moment. I shall also deal with Giles Florey. Leave a note on my dressing-table if you go out. Remember I'm still responsible for you, Gift or no Gift.'

So now Rosa was alone. Did Hetty want her to find The Gift? She wasn't sure.

*

Rosa went into the garden. It seemed alive with insects. Pollen-heavy bees buzzed through the scented air and a butterfly brushed against Rosa's cheek. A cloud of midges hung above the pond and metallic bluebottles crawled on the damp compost heap.

Broom lay purring in the shade of the apple tree with her silky paws outstretched. Rosa sat beside her and stroked her hot fur.

'How do I find a stone in a garden like this, Broom?' she said. 'Hetty threw it out of the door. It could have landed anywhere.'

Broom opened her eyes. She loved Rosa and could tell something was wrong. She climbed on to the girl's knee and snuggled up close, knowing that people usually liked this.

'Oh, you are a softy, Broom,' said Rosa.

The animal made her feel calm. She would find the stone if it was still in the garden.

'You'll have to get down, puss,' she said. 'I've got work to do.'

Rosa started near the back door and worked her way down the garden. The border was thick with marguerites, golden rod and tall echinops, hairy-stemmed geraniums, red hot pokers and bear's breeches. From what Rosa could see by peering or squeezing between them the soil was clear of stones, apart from the very tiny ones. She found that the rockeries by the east wall were made solely from large chunks of Cotswold stone, their gauntness softened by voluptuous trailing flowers, so she tackled the lawn next, pacing dizzily up and down it like a beetle until her dress began to stick to her. Then she laboriously checked Hetty's scree bed stone by stone. There were some beautiful ones of unusual shape and colour, but nothing like the stone in Florence Miller's picture. She flopped down under the apple tree again and lifted her damp hair off her neck. It seemed hopeless, but there was still the pond. She wouldn't bother with the vegetable patch. Hetty couldn't possibly have thrown it that far.

She heard a rustling noise from beside the pond and saw Broom's ears amongst the catmint.

'Broom,' she called sternly, 'you're not after Hetty's goldfish again, are you?'

Broom took no notice and slowly dipped her paw into the deep water, leaving it poised, a lethal scoop, waiting for its prey.

'You're not going to make me get up, are you?' said Rosa. 'You've *had* breakfast and I need a rest.'

Broom kept quite still as Rosa approached. She knew the fish couldn't resist coming up to sun themselves and could see the gleam of an appetizing one on the bed of the pond. If it would just swim near to her paw she'd have it. There was something nice about a meal that wriggled.

'I see it, Broom,' said Rosa. 'Let's hope it's seen you too, you naughty thing.'

A pair of newts touched the surface for air, floating with their legs outstretched for a while before kicking down into the weed. Snails laboured their way across the water between spinning whirligigs and darting boatmen. To Broom's irritation several goldfish wriggled up through a patch of blanket weed on the other side of the pond. She pulled out her wet paw, pushed her way awkwardly back through the catmint and padded round to the other side.

'You've met your match, Broom,' laughed Rosa.

She picked a reed and tickled the fish's side with it. It kept quite still at the base of the water plantain.

'Playing possum, are you?' said Rosa. She lowered her

'Yes?'

'Do you think Rod would drop us off at the coach station? I'd like to go over to Wescombe with you and Jamie again. I've got enough money left for the fares if I break into the emergency fund and Sharee could look after the dogs.'

Tom knew better than to ask why they were going.

TWENTY-TWO

Before she left the house Rosa wrote a note for Hetty in case Tom had missed her. Then she put the stone at the bottom of her canvas shoulder-bag, along with her purse, some paper tissues and a comb.

Rod Johnson took all of them to Sladbury, as hoped. Hetty sat in the front with him while Jake, Rosa, Tom and Jamie sat among paint tins and bags of tools in the back.

The boys had agreed not to question Rosa about The Gift but they soon guessed the truth. As Rod drove round the laborious bends on the outskirts of Sladbury, Rosa suddenly called out: 'Look out! There's something in the road.'

Rod braked immediately, but saw nothing until he slowly rounded the next sharp bend where, in the middle of the road, was a confused sheep.

'It's got through the fence,' said Rosa. 'I'll see it back in.'

She clambered out of the van, relieved to be out of the paint fumes for a while. The sheep stood wide-eyed and still as she approached, but it relaxed as soon as she touched its back.

'It's all right,' she whispered. 'I'll have you back in no time.'

She led it up the steep verge and pushed it through a broken fence panel, tapping it on its bottom to make it go into the field. She then asked the bemused Rod if she could borrow a hammer and some nails to sort the fence out.

'The girl's amazing,' he said, grinning incredulously. 'That animal followed her like a pet dog. And she's not bad at mending fences either. It's a good job she spotted the silly creature. We could have had a nasty accident there.'

Rod dropped Hetty and Jake at the police station first.

'Good luck, Jake,' said Tom.

'Good luck to you, too,' said Jake. But he was looking at Rosa.

'That sheep wasn't the only thing you found this morning, was it?' he said.

Rosa, Jamie and Tom travelled beyond Wescombe, this time to the village of Little Wescombe. Dilapidated cottages sat around a small bay. The beach was of pebbles and coarse sand with a curved spit of land to the northeast. Out to sea was the flat island from Florence Miller's painting.

'She must have lived along the front,' said Rosa. 'It's a pity we don't know the address.'

'One of the cottages has been done up,' said Jamie. 'It's a coffee shop, Amy Allsopp's Coffee House.'

'What a strange thing to find here,' said Tom.

'Let's go in for an early lunch,' said Jamie. 'I'm starving.'

It was a cosy place, with soft carpet, paintings on the wall and choice pot plants in little alcoves.

'Let's just have a sandwich and some squash,' said Rosa. 'It looks expensive and we may need the money for something else.'

'I'm skint,' said Jamie. 'I think I'll skip the squash.'

They sat at a polished wooden table and ordered from a pleasant grey-haired lady.

'Why have we come to a dump like Little Wescombe?' said Jamie, when she had gone.

'Because Florence Miller lived here, and so did Violet until she moved to Black Nest. I just wanted to get the feel of the place. I thought it might help me decide what to do. I wish I knew where they lived. I feel it must be very close. Look at the view. It's almost identical to the one in the painting.'

But Tom was staring intently at a picture on the wall behind Rosa. It was a seascape.

'Take a look at that,' he said. 'Recognize the style?'

It was unmistakable. The delicate brush strokes could have been the work of any excellent artist, but the grey sea was so subtly coloured that it seemed to move. Tom pushed his face nearer. In the corner of the painting, barely visible unless you were looking for it, were the initials *F. M.*

The lady brought the sandwiches. She smiled at them.

'I see you are admiring my painting,' she said. 'Exquisite, isn't it? It was painted by a lady who lived here many years ago.'

128

'Did she leave them to you?' asked Jamie.

'No. My mother found lots of them after she'd bought the place. They were in one of the outhouses along with a trunk full of painting equipment. Mother was surprised the former owner had left them. She was a young thing, going to Gloucestershire to get married. When she left she apologized for not clearing out the outbuildings. She said there was nothing she wanted from there and my mother could do what she liked with anything she found. Otherwise Mother would have contacted her, of course. I can't help feeling she didn't know they existed, though. There was a big lock on the door as if they had been stored in secret.'

'What an interesting story,' said Rosa. 'I don't suppose you can remember her name, can you?'

'I can, as a matter of fact. I looked it up last year. Her name was Violet Miller. I couldn't find her married name or the address she moved to, but she'll not be alive now.'

'What happened to the other pictures?' said Tom.

The woman sat down with them.

'I do love to talk to the customers,' she said happily. 'And I know the waitresses would rather I kept out of their way.'

Rosa was sure that there was nobody else in the building and certainly no waitresses.

'You were going to tell us about the paintings,' said Jamie.

'So I was. The American gentleman wanted her name. He was such a nice man. He came to talk about art at my women's group last summer and we each took a picture to show him. He loved mine. I told him I had lots more of them at home and he kindly offered to come and see them.

'It was lovely to have such an important visitor. I think

the other ladies were quite envious. He stayed all afternoon and wanted to know all about me. Before he left he asked me if I would like to sell any paintings. He said the artist was not known, but he thought he might get a modest price for them in America. I was quite surprised by his offer and wasn't sure I wanted to sell. I didn't look at the paintings often, but I loved every one of them, so I told him I couldn't part with them. I said that to me they were priceless.

'He was very disappointed, almost cross, and left quite promptly. It rather spoiled the evening. I thought that would be the end of it. He was due to return to America that month, having lectured at Bristol University for a summer course. But a week later he came to the door saying he'd considered what I had said and had arranged with his bank to give me a sum of money. I nearly fainted when he told me how much, but I still wasn't keen to sell. In the end we compromised. He rearranged the pictures on my walls and made suggestions as to how I could show them to their best advantage. I could soon see that I had had far too many up. By the time we'd finished I was left with the original box full and several others as well and not a place for them on the walls. His offer was so good I let him take the rest. As he said, "What's the point in owning something precious if you have to keep it hidden away?"'

'How did you feel about it afterwards?'

'Wonderful. I felt rich. The coffee shop was causing me some anxiety at the time. I don't make much of a profit, if any. I had my pension and some money my mother left me, but it wasn't quite enough. The extra money means I can run my little shop without worrying. Little Wescombe is hardly a major tourist attraction, but I do get to chat to a few people each week and that's good company.'

'How many pictures did you keep?' asked Rosa.

'Six in here and four upstairs. I kept my favourites, paintings of the estuary. They seemed to belong to the cottage. Mother said they were like a gift. I feel a bit sad about losing the others, but you can't really have three dozen pictures on your walls in a place like this.'

She stood up.

'I must be boring you to tears, and there's you trying to eat your sandwiches,' she said.

'Not at all,' said Tom.

'It was very interesting,' said Rosa.

'Bless you, dear. My waitress seems to be busy in the kitchen so I'll wheel over the sweet trolley. You must all have something gooey on the house. And you will call again, won't you?'

Later they walked along the pebbly beach.

'So Florence hid *her* talent as well,' said Jamie. 'She must have painted most of her pictures in secret. Fancy Violet not knowing there was a gold-mine in the outhouse.'

'Perhaps she did know,' said Rosa. 'But *A Gift from the Sea* was all she needed.'

'Why leave them there though? She could have given them to a gallery or something,' said Tom.

'Perhaps it was her mother's wish. We'll never know.'

'The Gift seems to make people do very odd things,' said Jamie.

'It's nice that Amy Allsopp's got her coffee shop,' said Rosa. 'But I can't help thinking of poor old Dora, with nothing to show for Florence's and Violet's talents.'

'She's got Black Nest,' said Tom. 'It's far too big for one, but her allowance is enough for her to stay there for as long as she wants.'

'It's friends she needs,' said Rosa. 'She's got that silly

dog now, but it's not the same. I think we ought to try to see her a bit more when we're here.'

'People *do* try,' said Jamie, 'but she won't let them in. Mum always makes sure she's OK when she takes her order, but she usually gets shouted at by Dora and barked at by the dog. Dora won't even let your Aunt Hetty in.'

'Makes you feel awful for calling her Dotty Dora, doesn't it?' said Rosa.

The tide had turned, but only the top of the beach was exposed. They climbed up on to a long wooden jetty and stared out to sea. On the water's edge an oyster-catcher turned pebbles with its long orange bill, searching for sand worms and tiny fish. It seemed surprisingly unperturbed by their presence. Waves lapped close to its legs, rattling loose pebbles.

'I found The Gift,' said Rosa eventually.

She gazed out over the grey water.

'I knew it!' said Jamie, slapping his leg enthusiastically. 'That sheep business was a dead give-away, and look at the way that penguin thing has come up to the jetty.'

'It's most powerful when I touch it,' she said. 'But the strength lingers on.'

'Great,' said Jamie. 'There'll be no stopping you now. You'll be famous!'

'What if someone finds out about The Gift?' said Rosa.

'How could they? Dora won't tell, Jake burned the diaries, and you know you can trust me, Tom and Hetty.'

A small boat chugged towards the jetty, bobbing the gulls that sat on the water.

'What do *you* think, Tom?'

He said nothing. His face clouded.

'Tell me,' whispered Rosa. 'I need to know.'

The boat slid up against the jetty, barking its hull. An old man with a weathered face climbed slowly from it and tied it up. The name on the side was faded but familiar.

IVY WOTHERS

''Ello,' said the man. 'Nice drop of weather we've got today, isn't it? I like a bit of a breeze. You can keep your sunshine. Gives me 'eadaches, it does.'

'Been fishing, have you?' said Tom.

'No. I haven't the patience these days. Me joints get to ache a bit if I stay on the water for too long. I just like to go round the island and back on me better days.'

'I like the name of your boat,' said Rosa.

'It's the name of a dear old lady as used to tell fortunes in Wescombe. Granddaughter of Neptune the Magnificent. I don't expect you've 'eard of 'im, but round 'ere he was reckoned to be more than a bit special. Ivy Wothers was quite a girl too so I thought I'd name me boat after her. Why aren't you in Wescombe? Nobody comes here. Specially not kids.'

'We fancied a change,' said Tom.

'We've been to the coffee shop,' said Rosa.

'She makes me laugh, does Amy Allsopp. Has a coffee shop here of all places, with posh wallpaper a mile thick and real wood tables. She tries to entice me in there but I tell 'er me boots would spoil the carpet. Goodness knows what she does with the leftover food. She can hardly 'ave more than a couple of customers a day.'

'I like it here,' said Rosa.

The man looked pleased.

Tom and Jamie looked less enthusiastic.

'Give me a ride in your boat?' she said. 'Just round the island and back.'

'Rosa!' said Tom. 'You can't ask a stranger to give you lifts.'

'Come with me then.'

133

'Count me out,' said Jamie. 'Boats make my gut go funny.'

'I think someone's opinion 'as been forgot,' said the man. 'Who says I'm prepared to give lifts to any Tom, Dick or Harriet who comes along?'

'Please,' said Rosa. 'It's important. We'll pay you of course.'

Tom looked worried. They only just had enough money left for the fare home.

'Wouldn't dream of letting you pay,' he said. 'Never been called mean, I 'aven't. Hop in.'

The salt air moistened their faces as they lurched towards the island.

'The island's full of birds,' said the man. 'Cormorants, puffins and that.'

A gull swooped very close to the boat so that Rosa felt the air rush past her cheek.

'Them gulls are getting a bit bold,' said the man. 'But I've never 'ad one as close as that. Mind if I sing? I likes to sing a song out here.'

He sang a song about the fish of the sea, and while he sang the children talked.

'Why have we come?' said Tom.

'I wanted to talk to you alone.'

'We're hardly alone. What about the old chap?'

'He's not listening to us. You must tell me what you think about The Gift. I need help and you know me best.'

'Not any more,' said Tom.

'What do you mean?'

'It's just that you're not *you* any more,' he said. His voice was fierce and Rosa knew he was close to tears. 'You've always been a bit odd with animals, but this is different . . .'

'But it's not a *bad* thing, Tom. You know I'd only use it for good.'

'You don't know what it might do to you. It got to work on your mind before you'd even heard of it. Remember the nightmares. *They* weren't good.'

'The Gift scares me, Tom, but Connie wanted me to have it.'

'Florence wanted Violet to have it, but what good did it do her? She had to hide away in the loft and deceive her daughter.'

'She did make a lot of money for charity.'

'I don't care about *her*. It's you I'm worried about. You asked what I thought and I've told you, but it's you who has to decide.'

The man stopped singing.

'We're coming round the island now,' he said. 'The water's at its deepest here.'

Rosa heard the shrieking of birds.

'I didn't expect them to be so loud,' she shouted.

'Your hearing must be better than mine,' said the man. 'I can't hear them yet.'

The water was more exposed now and the boat rocked up and down.

Rosa began to feel dizzy . . .

And when she looked at the water the surface was crowded with the gaping mouths of a thousand fish. Their urgent bodies bumped against the side of the boat as if they would pound a hole in it.

Then she saw a low black cloud over the island, and as the cloud moved towards them she saw that it was a mass of wheeling, screeching birds. Now the birds were above them and it was as dark as twilight.

Rosa reached in her canvas bag and drew out the stone. She gripped it firmly with both hands and felt its strength surge through her . . .

*

Birds shrieked. Fish gaped. The boat rocked. And then the voices came.

> 'What does he want, Dora? Why is he coming? You must tell me . . . you trust your Connie, don't you?'
>
> 'Take The Gift, Connie, and the letter . . . I'm scared . . . I shouldn't have taken your present . . . Mummy wanted **you** to have it . . . help me, Connie . . .'
>
> 'It's all right, Dora . . . you've told me now. Let me hold it. Then I'll understand . . .'
>
> 'Have it . . . **Take it!** . . . I can hear him on the roof. Look out of the skylight. It's him . . . He's seen us! . . . **Go away, nasty man!**'
>
> 'Quickly, Dora . . . we must go down . . . **Quickly!**'
>
> 'Connie, wake up. Where does it hurt? **Wake up!**'

The birds were thick above them now like a black canopy. And Rosa heard Ivy's voice.

> 'It's in safe hands . . . but she doesn't understand the dangers.'
>
> 'Give it to her when she's ready, Hetty . . . she'll know what to do . . .'
>
> 'Neptune was wrong . . . **wrong** . . . sometimes a gift is not a gift.'

The fish pushed their heads right out of the water now, and the birds flapped so close that Rosa thought she might suffocate. She could see the stone in her hands. The blue crystals sparkled. The amber gleamed. She drew back her arm and felt the weight of the stone for the last time. As she hurled it from the boat the birds and fish were gone. She watched it streak through the air in an arc of amber.

136

When it touched the surface of the water it seemed to rest there for a second, as if supported by a hand. Then it sank into the deep sea.

Tom was crouching in the bottom of the boat, his face horrified, but the man started singing again as if nothing had happened.

'It's all right, Tom,' she said. 'It's gone. It won't hurt anybody now.'

They sat close together until the boat reached the jetty.

'Thank you for the ride,' said Rosa.

'That's all right, me dear.'

Jamie called them from the road: 'Come on! There's a bus in five minutes.'

The man secured his boat and stared out to sea for a moment.

'We'd better be off, then,' said Tom.

He trudged up the beach; his legs felt heavy and his body weak with relief.

Rosa stayed with the man.

'What's the name of the island, then?' she asked.

'It's Stone Holme on the map, but the locals call it Black Nest, on account of all the birds.'

'That's an unusual name.'

The man nodded. He looked different now – taller and younger.

'You *must* have seen what happened out there,' she said. 'You did, didn't you?'

'Maybe,' he said. His voice was deeper, almost refined.

The boys called, but Rosa felt reluctant to leave.

'I'm Rosa,' she said. 'Who are you?'

'They used to call me "Neptune the Magnificent, Master of Prediction and Illusion",' he said. '*This* is nothing. I did some wonderful things in my time.'

He grandly twisted the end of an imaginary moustache.

For a moment he seemed tall and straight. Magnificent.
Then the vision was gone, the illusion faded, and he was
the villager again.

But this time he seemed older. Sadder.

'Even the magnificent make mistakes,' he said.

By the time Rosa reached the boys, both man and boat
were gone.